# THE MAGIC CIRCLE

# THE MAGIC CIRCLE

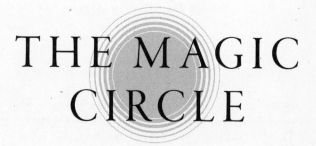

## JENNY DAVIDSON

NEW HARVEST

HOUGHTON MIFFLIN HARCOURT

*Boston   New York*   2013

This edition published by special arrangement with Amazon Publishing

For information about permission to reproduce selections from this book,
write to Permissions, Houghton Mifflin Harcourt Publishing Company,
215 Park Avenue South, New York, New York 10003.

www.hmhbooks.com

*Library of Congress Cataloging-in-Publication Data*
Davidson, Jenny.
The magic circle / Jenny Davidson.
pages  cm
ISBN 978-0-544-02809-8 (pbk.)
1. Female friendship — Fiction. 2. Gambling — Fiction. I. Title.
PS3604.A9467M34 2013
813'.6 — dc23
2012042638

Printed in the United States of America
DOC 10 9 8 7 6 5 4 3 2 1

*For Brent*

All play moves and has its being within a play-ground marked off beforehand either materially or ideally, deliberately or as a matter of course. Just as there is no formal difference between play and ritual, so the "consecrated spot" cannot be formally distinguished from the play-ground. The arena, the card-table, the magic circle, the temple, the stage, the screen, the tennis court, the court of justice, etc., are all in form and function play-grounds, i.e. forbidden spots, isolated, hedged round, hallowed, within which special rules obtain. All are temporary worlds within the ordinary world, dedicated to the performance of an act apart.

— JOHAN HUIZINGA, *Homo Ludens: A Study of the*
*Play-Element in Culture*

You do not know what your life is, or what you do, or who you are.

— Dionysus to Pentheus; EURIPIDES,
*The Bacchae,* trans. John Davie

# THE MAGIC CIRCLE

# TRAPPED IN THE ASYLUM

YOU: the most junior reporter at the *New York Tribune*. It's September 1882 and you've received a coveted special assignment: infiltrate the Bloomingdale Insane Asylum and report on conditions from the inside!

How you get there:

*Read up on current theories of insanity.*

*Choose a popular diagnosis: mania attributed to sunstroke?*

*Simulate the symptoms you've read about, then write to a friend to report you've been ill.*

*Document every detail of your condition in a mountain of paper.*

You check into a hotel downtown. Three days later, your behavior has begun to worry the management. Your dear friend and college classmate Mr. H——, concerned about your condition (really he is in on the secret), finds a doctor to visit you and make an assessment.

(You have enlisted the support of two trusted friends in character roles: aforementioned comrade H——, but also Y——, an out-of-work actor you met at a bar on the Bowery, who will pretend to be your uncle, with the authority to commit you to the asylum and the financial wherewithal to settle your bills in advance.)

The hotel proprietor secures the services of a male nurse to prevent you from leaving the room and frightening the other guests.

When H—— comes with the doctor, you spring up from your couch of repose and fling yourself towards the medical man. He recoils in terror.

The second doctor who enters is an altogether hardier soul. He consults with the nurse and is more satisfied than surprised to discover that your symptoms cannot be attributed to the excessive consumption of alcohol, none having made its way into the room over the past twenty-four hours. Your "uncle" is here now too, and shows himself thoroughly alarmed by your demeanor. He is ready to put up the dollars for what seems your only recourse: *commitment to the Bloomingdale Asylum for the Insane*. . . .

Both doctors appear in police court, where the justice issues forth an affidavit that permits your uncle to have you arrested and committed to an asylum within the city limits.

You are placed in a carriage whose driver transports you far uptown to Morningside Heights and the cool, clean, elevated, healthful environs of the Asylum. You submit to a brief—a very brief—examination by the chief doctor, who commits you to the care of a thuggish-looking and odorous attendant; the doors close behind you, an unutterable chill descends. . . .

• • •

They stood and gazed at the red brick house. Angular and stark in appearance, Buell Hall was the only building on the Columbia University campus to survive from the era of the Bloomingdale Asylum. Would there once have been trees around it, or was the effect of nakedness deliberate, strategic? It seemed to stand apart from the other buildings, contemptuous of newcomers, its sash windows staring blankly outwards in the late-afternoon light.

Ruth tapped a note into her iPhone.

"Go round to the other side. Could you have seen the river from there, do you think, before those buildings went up along the Broadway side of campus?"

Lucy stood where Ruth told her to.

"Hard to tell," she said. "I'm pretty sure you could have seen the bluffs on the New Jersey side, but there's a sharp enough dip from here down to the water that I would think the river itself might not have been visible. We should go inside and check out the view from that top window."

Ruth went around to the door on the other side of the building, but it was locked.

Anna had watched the proceedings curiously. As Ruth re-emerged, shaking her head, Anna mounted the bottom stairs of the fire escape that ran along the back wall.

"Be careful!" Lucy shouted.

The stairs ran directly from the ground, and no athleticism was required to begin the upward climb, but when Anna reached the top landing, she didn't just lean out and peer around the edge of the building, as Lucy had expected. Instead, she climbed onto the ledge that rimmed the roof's south side and began to walk sideways along it.

"What are you doing?" Ruth hissed, looking around to make sure no campus police were in sight. "Get down from there!"

Lucy had a great fear of heights.

"Tell me when she's back down on the ground again," she muttered, turning away from the building, hunching her face and shoulders down over her chest and covering up her eyes.

"It's perfectly safe," Anna called down. She had reached the end of the ledge at the building's southwest corner and stood up straight, hand shading her eyes. "I'm guessing that if the sightlines were clear, I'd be able to see the water. Perhaps only a glimpse, though, not a proper view."

"Get down, Anna!" Ruth called to her again. "You're going to get us all in trouble!"

Anna laughed, and danced lightly back along the ledge as if it were only three feet above the ground, not three full stories.

"She's on the fire escape now, Lucy," Ruth reported. "You can open your eyes."

Lucy opened her eyes and Anna was on the ground again, brushing the dirt off her coat and picking up the orange nylon messenger bag she'd dumped on the ground before making her ascent.

"I know something you don't," Anna said complacently. "It doesn't matter whether or not you can see the river."

"Why not?" said Ruth.

"Because in the days of the old asylum, this building used to stand on 116th Street. It was physically moved later on, to make way for Kent Hall."

"Why didn't you say so before?" Ruth asked. "How the hell am I supposed to evoke a historically authentic sense of place? It's the only obvious structure to build the game around, but if the building's in the wrong place, I might as well give up right now."

"Don't be a baby," Lucy said. "You want to capture the flavor of the past, but it doesn't have to be the exact literal truth, does it?"

"It might work better if it's not the literal truth," said Anna.

"Fact is always preferable to fiction," Ruth said. "Lucy, do you want to stop at home before we go to the bar?"

"I don't think so. Watching Anna about to fall to her death has given me the urge to have a drink as soon as possible."

Ruth and Lucy shared a university-owned apartment on the south side of West 122nd Street between Broadway and Amsterdam. A native New Yorker, Ruth had an undergraduate degree from Bryn Mawr and a PhD from NYU in game theory and design, and she now received housing as a postdoctoral fellow at the humanities center. She rented her second bedroom to Lucy at a very reasonable rate, a rate that Lucy was nonetheless barely able to afford after two years of full-time tuition as an MFA student at Columbia's School of the Arts. Anna had moved in down the hall at the end of the summer; a Copenhagen-based sociologist, she had received a Fulbright to study New York City's cultures of urban exploration.

At the bar, ten blocks south of campus on Amsterdam, Lucy ordered a microbrew and an all-beef hot dog. Anna asked for a vodka tonic, while Ruth ordered a glass of sauvignon blanc.

Once they had placed their order, Anna dug a scroll of papers from her bag and unrolled it onto the table in front of her. The top sheet was a map of Morningside Heights: not present-day Morningside Heights, but rather the area as it had been before the build-up that began around the turn of the last century. The map's delicate lines gave it a fantastical quality. The Hudson River bounded the neighborhood along the western edge, with the green strip of Riverside Park as a decorative border. Up above was Riverside Drive, separated from park and river by a natural cliff and a boundary wall of schist. To the east, Morningside Drive marked the top of another cliffside plummet down to the canyon of Morningside Park. Grant's Tomb was stationed like a gigantic brioche at the northwest corner of the neighborhood just before another natural drop-off, the geological plateau giving the whole area a fort-like quality. It could have been suitably defended by brightly clad Playmobil knights with trebuchets and caldrons of boiling oil to tip down on assailants below, with the Cathedral of St. John the Divine tucked beautifully catty-corner from Grant's Tomb to secure the final point of the fortification.

"I hadn't realized it was so empty in those days," said Lucy. "There were hardly any buildings to speak of, were there? It's strange. It's not that long ago, really."

Anna let the top sheet roll itself closed to uncover another page beneath. "Here's a map of the Bloomingdale Asylum around 1890," she said. "You can see the buildings and paths take up a very similar area to what's now the college's main quadrangle."

Ruth leaned over to look. Dusk had fallen, and the room was dim. She picked up the newly lit candle in its glass sheath and held it to shed a circle of light over the relevant sector.

"That's an amazing list of buildings in the legend on the side!" she said. "Laundry, bakeshop and boiler room; blacksmith and carpentry shops, a conservatory and stables and barns and even a gymnasium and bowling alley. The asylum was really its own self-enclosed little world, like a medieval monastery."

"Look," Anna said, putting her finger to the spot, "here's the porter's lodge. That's the obvious spot for players to begin."

Lucy enjoyed the sight of Anna and Ruth alongside one another, their heads bent over the map like two figures cast from the same mold, then finished by different brushes after emerging from the kiln. Anna was dark-haired, ringleted, slim, her spoken English precise and so little accented that only its hyper-correctness spoke to her foreign origin. She was the granddaughter of Greek immigrants to Sweden, but the Greek national particularities she might have been expected to exhibit seemed to have been eradicated by the juggernaut of Swedish linguistic and cultural homogeneity. Ruth's hair was dark like Anna's but straight and shoulder length, blunt cut, her figure as compact and delicate as an eighteenth-century snuffbox, her small pale face unmemorable except when animation made it briefly exquisite.

*Trapped in the Asylum* would form a companion project to the book Ruth was working on, *Think Global/Play Local!,* a project that had been endlessly described at parties and earned her all sorts of grants and accolades but that Lucy worried might never actually be written, Ruth being so much more passionate about the games themselves than about their theorization and/or narrative chronicling. Lucy was herself the "published author" — a phrase she mentally sandwiched in mocking air-quotes — of chapbooks titled *Physical Chemistry* and *The Submersibles,* as well as some dozen poems in literary journals, but each individual thing she wrote felt small, a single tile rather than a complete mosaic, and it had yet to seem real to her that any cumulative life's work of substance would emerge from future years of writing and publishing. Her father, a Taiwanese American engineer, had died of pancreatic cancer when Lucy was a teenager, and Lucy felt herself to be still somehow provisional, uncommitted to life and its full unfolding.

"How many of these buildings are still standing?" Ruth asked Anna, who had been the one to mine the archives for the old maps.

"Buell Hall's really the only one. Almost every other trace has been erased, at least above ground. There will be some remnants below; the present-day tunnels were built into the nineteenth-century system."

"I'm not sure how that will suit my purposes," said Ruth, frowning. "The educational component of this project is important to me. I want to give these kids a real sense of the neighborhood at different times in its history, and it's no good if they can't see old buildings. It leaves too much to the imagination. Maybe I should be thinking bigger? Not just the asylum, but the whole history of the neighborhood right up through the 1940s?"

"Suit yourself," Anna said with a shrug. "I would start small, myself. There's not much point expanding the game to the whole of Morningside Heights until you've established a suitable array of technological and ludic mechanisms for the smaller footprint. The idea of the asylum nicely focuses the game's interest."

The phrase "ludic mechanisms" sounded preposterous to Lucy — to use a word like *ludic* leached too much of the playfulness out of play — but Anna's advice was otherwise sensible. Ruth was frequently confounded by the grand scope of her own projects and the difficulty inhering in their ever being successfully executed.

"Let's say you go with the asylum premise," Lucy said, rotating the map 180 degrees so that she could look at it right side up. "You could teach the kids about the history of psychiatric treatment in the United States, about architecture, about urban planning, about the sociology of small communities...."

"Yes, exactly," said Ruth triumphantly. She volunteered several mornings a week at a local high school, and the game was part of her larger mission to convert educators into believers in the value of locative games. "I think it could work!"

Anna was flagging down the waitress. Ruth hadn't yet finished her first drink, so Anna ordered a second vodka for herself and another pint of pale ale for Lucy, who was trying to keep an eye on her alcohol intake and had regretfully deemed beer's caloric overload preferable to the moral hazard of excessive whisky consumption.

"Is 'cub reporter with an investigative mission' really an adequate premise?" Anna asked.

"I think it's better than adequate," Ruth said, bristling. "The material's drawn from a great book that Lucy found, a contemporary tell-all exposé by a guy called Julius Chambers, so we can be sure it's reasonably authentic. It highlights interesting aspects of the social history of the era, and it paves the way for the kids to ask all sorts of questions. They can do library research to supplement the points they get by picking up virtual objects or bits of information within the game itself."

Anna looked amused, but said nothing.

"What?" Ruth asked, sensitive to the slightest hint of criticism.

"It's just that none of this seems very imaginative," Anna said. "It could be so much darker, more intense: the ghosts of dead madmen shaped by the torment of treatments undergone at the hands of the doctors of that era, the sinister specter of nineteenth-century medical experimentation, perhaps even a killer stalking the hallways. Your game-players might like to experience something of a gothic *frisson*."

"They are *children!*" Ruth exclaimed, her voice rising. "I don't want to fill them up with ridiculous made-up ideas about the past. I want them to learn about *history!*"

"Notions of haunting and possession persist across many cultures," Anna said. "I am not superstitious myself, but it would be obtuse to disregard the possibility of their having some deeper cognitive and spiritual basis. I'd say it's actively self-defeating to keep your game so thoroughly in the mundane world."

The two had rehearsed versions of this argument before, and Lucy felt herself withdraw both intellectually and emotionally. She hated arguments. When the waitress came back with their drinks, Lucy took a deep swallow, then deposited the glass back down on the table and crossed her arms over her chest in a sort of protective barrier.

"You and I have totally different understandings of what a game is," Ruth told Anna. Her cheeks were pink, and her voice had become bossier, more nitpicky. "You're talking about games like they're some sort of dark instrument of counter-enlightenment, but for me, they're magical precisely because they're so rational. They can be used for pedagogical purposes, to build up cognitive skills, to recreate lost worlds. Of course there's an imaginative component here: I want the kids to be transported, but the world they go to is going to be as real as I can make it. The rules of physics will apply there, and so will the real facts of history, with no anachronisms or anomalies."

Anna shook her head.

"Even a self-evidently rational game like chess," she said softly, "releases certain energies, emotions, and passions that can't be explained in altogether rational terms. Games that take place inside a magic circle make strange things happen."

"What is a magic circle?" Lucy asked.

"You're just being disingenuous," Ruth snapped. "Don't change the subject. I'm sick of the way you always try to stave off confrontation."

"No, I really don't know," said Lucy.

"It could be a sacred grove or just the space in which a game is played," Anna said. "Even an ordinary childhood game like sardines turns a house into a magic circle. The circle might be a boxing ring or a sports arena. It's just a way of talking about an amoeba-shaped space of play, one that's distinctly demarcated from the ordinary world outside. Whatever happens within the magic circle is fundamentally discontinuous with the external world."

"But it need not be magical in the literal sense. It's magical only in that it differs from the mundane," Ruth persisted. "Games don't have to be fantastical to be good. You yourself admit boxing as an example."

"You two are never going to be able to make a decisive determination of the respective merits of fact and fantasy," Lucy said. "Can't we talk about something else?"

Ruth still looked temper-stricken, but Anna started to laugh.

"Quite right," she said. "I am certainly very happy to have been able to find you these materials, Ruth, regardless of what you choose to do with them."

"And I will keep on helping with the research," said Lucy. She had written the first mock-up of game text already, her genuine interest augmented by Ruth's readiness to accept hours of Lucy's time in lieu of some portion of next month's rent. It might be true what Anna said, though: Lucy could feel in herself something of a yen for the irrational to creep in, something strange, something uncanny, even perhaps something actually mad. It would be ironic, in a pitiful way, if *Trapped in the Asylum* should turn out to have the sanitized texture and flavor of, say, a hot dog bun as opposed to the yeasty wildness of sourdough.

## ANNA'S APHORISMS

---

### Dangerous games

October 8, 2010; 12:53 a.m.

What I learned from R. the other day: a distinction between games that are inherently dangerous and games that are merely contingently so. (The gladiator's severed hand as opposed to the soccer player's torn ligament.) Not inherently dangerous, though every game has the potential for danger: *invisible theater,* political drama performed in a public space without visible labels, a performance that lures unwitting onlookers to participate. Dangerous as part of its actual rationale: *dark play,* in which some players may not even know that they are playing a game. A classic example: Russian roulette in traffic, players crossing streets without looking and drivers drawn unwittingly into becoming players; a violent and consequential form of play, one that leaves a significant proportion of players ignorant of the very fact of the game.

*Posted in* Danger, Games, Ignorance, Theater, Traffic

"A pocketknife," Ruth said firmly. "It can be dug up from a hiding place in the vegetable garden, and it will allow the player to cut through the door of her cell to access the keyhole — escape isn't guaranteed, but it's a necessary first step."

Lucy was sitting by the big computer on the dining table while Ruth lay on her back on the couch, feet resting over its arm and laptop balanced on her stomach.

Lucy added *pocketknife* to the list. It hadn't been hard to come up with a longish list of virtual objects for the players of *Trapped in the Asylum* to collect. The things fell into two main categories: items to aid escape or investigation (pen and paper, a postage stamp, a prepaid telegram form) and items to console or comfort (a bar of chocolate, fresh bed linens, clean underwear). Objects in the first category would be hidden in preset locations to which the players would be guided by geographical puzzles, questions and clues, while objects in the second category would be awarded following the successful completion of various research tasks.

Ruth had modeled this aspect of *Trapped* on a popular Japanese game called Mogi, in which players collected virtual objects with their mobile phones, each object belonging to a different collection and with points accruing on the basis of completing individual collections. The mobile device of choice was the iPhone; Ruth's last few games had been conducted on a range of phones and personal digital assistants, and one drawer in the living room tallboy was jammed with old Nokias and Palms, but the GPS feature on the Apple product was so easy to use — and the device itself so all-pervasive in the collegiate environment — that it seemed the inevitable vanquisher of all competition.

Much of the game content had been mined from a fascinating nonfiction account by the nineteenth-century muckraking journalist Julius Chambers; it had initially been published as a series of articles in the *Herald Tribune,* appearing shortly thereafter in book form. As Ruth conceived it, each potential player would receive an invitation to participate in *Trapped in the Asylum* in the form of a reproduction of the original telegram Chambers' editor had sent him: "Will you feign insanity; enter Doctor B——'s madhouse as a patient, and write an exposé?" She had photoshopped it from a scanned version of a real late-nineteenth-century telegram scavenged from a box of architectural records at Avery Library; the page of the telegram then dissolved and the text providing backstory and setup scrolled down the screen. Though it remained at its heart Ruth's personal project, Lucy had very thoroughly entered into the spirit of *Trapped,* even enlisting her class of first-year undergraduate writing students to test some of the applications Ruth had devised.

"How do you get the player to the correct real-world starting spot, though?" Lucy asked. "You've placed the fictional protagonist actually *in* the asylum by the end of that bit, but you haven't built in a way to get the player to Buell Hall or wherever will be the point of departure."

"The first thing I want the player to do is look beyond what's currently there — the Columbia campus — and discern the terrain of the early 1880s," Ruth said. "The natural starting point is determined by the present-day configuration, inevitably, so I imagine the player begins at 116th Street and Broadway, at the 1 train entrance just by the main gates."

"The player's standing with her device at 116th and Broadway," Lucy agreed. "She's got her iPhone out; she's already received the invitation and read the backstory. What then?"

"We've got to roll back a few weeks earlier," Ruth mused. "An initial assessment of the lay of the land. Stage one of the game. . . ."

Lucy opened the folder on the computer that held all of the images they had obtained. A cluster of late-nineteenth-century maps showed the locations of the original asylum buildings, the walks and gardens surrounding the buildings, and so forth. The archives were full of photographs as well: the central building was a brownstone leviathan that had begun by being stately but grew increasingly shabby as the century progressed and wings were built onto it piecemeal. Visual texturing would be achieved by overlaying these images on ones from the present; maps and aerial photographs did the critical work of orientation, while the player subsequently had only to turn in a new direction with the phone and take a picture with the camera accessory within the game app to pull up a late-nineteenth-century image taken from a similar spot and angle.

Ruth had farmed out the work of organizing the photographs and orienting them to the points of the compass to a very smart computer science graduate student called Tim, whose passion for Ruth, though it did not seem likely to be requited, made him receptive to her regular requests for help. Ruth was a more than competent programmer herself, but she had learned to delegate whatever she could to researchers and developers, game design being a time-suck on the same order as filmmaking or live theater. Lucy often experienced sneaking relief that she had no particular technical know-how, as even the limited help she could offer with research and writing left her feeling drained.

"The camera will have two main functions," Ruth stated, Lucy adding a note to the instructions: "aerial, which will switch back and forth between cartographic and photographic modes in something like a gradual fade, and on-ground. But I also want a geological mode. The features of the constructed landscape owe so much to the underlying terrain, the students will be missing out if they don't get a bit of earth science here too."

"They get that with a separate instrument, maybe? A surveying tool of some kind?"

"Yes, but it's mapmaking basically, so it still should be integrated with the aerial view."

Lucy clicked on the subfolder dedicated to geological maps. She liked earth science and it had been easy to write the description of the terrain, a legend that emphasized the topographic isolation of Morningside Heights on the rocky plateau rising above the Harlem Plain. Only about two thousand feet separated the cliffs of Riverside from those of Morningside, with the intervening strip of land forming a section of the Manhattan Ridge, made primarily of mica. The area had remained relatively rural right up to the end of the nineteenth century. The elevation had made it expensive and undesirable to extend the railroads up the western side of the island, with trains instead running into northern Manhattan through the flatter terrain of central Harlem. The Broadway subway didn't open until 1903, at which point the neighborhood finally did fall into the hands of the real-estate developers who went on to construct the upper-middle-class apartment buildings that gave the neighborhood its strongly residential character.

"Are you at all tempted to introduce some more theatrical component?" Lucy asked. "You know, like maybe an actor playing a villainous attendant to serve as gatekeeper, or a telegraph operator who would actually take a message and send it?"

"When larping is done well, it can be completely magical," Ruth said, "but when it's done badly, it ruins the seriousness of the game."

"Larping," Lucy mused, chewing over the word in her mouth. "Live-action role-playing?"

"It's a pretty goofy-sounding word, isn't it? I remember one time during the Tetragrammaton game in Minneapolis, we had to wait for two hours because the bartender who was supposed to give you a secret clue if you ordered a cocktail called the Oxford blue had changed shifts with a co-worker without notifying the game master. Another time my friend Mitch gave CPR to a girl he thought was just pretending to have a heart attack, but it turned out she was having a real one."

"As long as it was real CPR," Lucy said.

"I guess it's hard for me to give up the degree of control that would be entailed in allowing other people to play live parts in the game," said Ruth. "The devices are entirely within my domain. I can determine each player's experience within certain clearly defined boundaries, and players can enjoy the game on their own time and at any hour of day or night. Introducing actors risks things getting much sillier, and of course harder to coordinate."

They were interrupted by Anna's knock at the door. Her arrival tipped the evening over from work to revelry. Lucy shut down the computer and Ruth gathered up papers and assembled them in tidy piles before going to the kitchen. She emerged some minutes later with little bowls of snacks (briny olives, salted almonds), three wineglasses, and a bottle of red, which she opened, capably, with a waiter's corkscrew.

"Lucy, if you prefer white, there's a bottle already open in the fridge," she said, pouring glasses of Malbec for herself and Anna.

Lucy did prefer white, and went to get some. When she came back into the living room, Anna was looking amused as Ruth — ethnographically, with condescension — informed her that young girls in America, holding sleepovers at one another's houses, often played a game called truth or dare.

"What's to stop us from playing it now?" Anna said immediately. "We have a similar game in Sweden, I think. It is called *Sanning eller konsekvens,* truth or consequences."

Lucy was a physical coward and hated to be embarrassed. She had always chosen the truth option as a child, even when her friends groaned and begged her to take dare for a change. It had never been a favorite game with her; surely it was a game for those who dared rather than those with secrets?

"Yes, let's play!" said Ruth.

Lucy looked at her, surprised. It was true that Ruth loved games of all sorts, but it was more like her to suggest some unusual board game or intricate pencil-and-paper routine than to court more extreme forms of physical or emotional risk-taking. It must be that Anna's presence worked as a catalyst.

The first few rounds were mostly in the nature of getting the feel of things. Ruth chose dare, and Anna challenged her to run down to the lobby and back up all six flights of stairs in her bra and underpants; this was exactly the sort of challenge that made Lucy cringe in aversion, but Ruth (who was very fit and slender, and who had attended a girls' school that inoculated her against all the major strains of teasing and female devilry) just kicked off her house shoes, pulled the charcoal viscose jersey dress off over her head, tugged down the leggings she was wearing underneath and left the heap of clothes in a pile on the floor, returning breathless and pink-faced some minutes later.

"Your turn, Lucy," said Ruth, clad again now and refreshing herself with a slug of wine. "Truth or dare?"

"Truth," Lucy said fervently, feeling an utter coward.

Ruth looked at Anna, then at Lucy.

"Between me and Anna," she said, a smile sneaking onto her face, "which of us would you rather sleep with?"

Lucy blushed a deep brick red.

"Ummmm," she said, "you are both very attractive, but. . . ."

The truth was that she found Ruth sexually sterile, pretty but neuter in the feelings she prompted unless you counted as some kind of sexual displacement the sort of passionate irritation one sometimes felt towards a close friend and roommate, whereas Anna was irresistible, even to someone like Lucy at the straight end of the spectrum.

"Say it," Ruth commanded.

"I would have sex with Anna," Lucy confessed.

"I knew it!" Ruth cried out, sounding strangely pleased.

"I will take it as a compliment," Anna said, smiling.

"Anna, your turn again now," Ruth said. "Truth or dare?"

She was ringleading, Lucy thought.

"Dare, of course," Anna said, laughing. "I am curious to hear how you will revenge yourself!"

After a pause in which Lucy anxiously contemplated what form the dare might take, Ruth cried out, "I have a good one! Anna,

I dare you to go back to your apartment, climb out through the window and reenter our apartment through the kitchen window. I will go and open it for you now, no housebreaking skills required."

"You can't make her do that," Lucy objected. "There's no fire escape on that side of the building. We're six floors up!"

"Yes, the same six flights she made me run half-naked," Ruth agreed smugly. "It's not dangerous, really. I know Anna has done a ton of climbing."

Anna had already stood up and was flexing her hands and wrists. She was smiling; the absence of any tension in her body language made Lucy give a low moan, cover up her eyes and shrink down onto the couch, as if the fetal position would somehow protect them all from the impending danger.

"Lucy, you have to come and see this!" Ruth called out from her spot by the kitchen window.

"I can't!" Lucy shouted back. "I really can't bear to watch. Is she actually crawling around the outside of the building?"

"She's made it halfway already," Ruth said. "She makes it look like the easiest thing in the world!"

As much as it filled her with dread, Lucy gave in and joined Ruth in the kitchen. Ruth had pulled up the screen and was leaning out to watch; even that made Lucy wildly anxious, and when she stood behind Ruth and leaned her own head out, she was afraid she was going to be sick.

Anna was standing on a small ledge, the top lintel of the window a floor below, inching her way along; she reached the end and went into a kind of triangle pose, reaching out with her left foot to the bottom edge of the next window, getting a good foothold there and then spinning in that direction almost as if she were about to do a cartwheel. Intermediate hand- and footholds were offered by the protruding bits of brick that were a decorative feature of the building's facade, but it took Lucy's breath away to see how far down the ground was.

Anna was almost there. Lucy pulled Ruth back from the window.

"Give her plenty of room to get in," she gasped. "I can hardly stand it!"

A minute later, after the sound of scrambling, Ruth was laughing and pulling Lucy's hands down from where they covered her eyes.

"You can look now," Anna said, brushing the scuff mark off one knee of her black jeans and flexing her forearms. "I need to climb more often. Even that short traverse got me pumped!"

"There is a climbing wall in the gym at Chelsea Piers," Ruth suggested.

"Indoor climbing is too tame," said Anna.

Back in the living room, they drank more wine and embarked on another round of the game. Ruth gave a comical and somewhat truth-deflecting answer to Anna's question about how she had lost her virginity, and Lucy a comical and more deeply confessional account of the time she was caught shoplifting as a teenager and had her picture taken for the Polaroid wall of shame behind the counter at Urban Outfitters.

Anna again: this time the foreigner chose truth, Ruth deferring to Lucy vis-à-vis the formulation of an appropriate question.

"I can't think of anything!" Lucy protested.

"Yes, you can," Ruth said.

"What's the worst thing that ever happened to you?" Lucy said finally, unable to come up with anything more pointed or humorous.

"The worst thing that ever happened to me?" Anna said, taken aback.

"Yes, the worst thing that ever happened to you."

"It is a question that requires some thought."

"Requires some thought because nothing much bad has happened to you," asked Ruth, reaching over to pour the last of the red into Anna's glass, "or because so many bad things have happened to you that it's hard to narrow it down to only one?"

Anna didn't answer Ruth directly.

"Most people," she said slowly, "would probably say the worst thing that ever happened to me was spending two years in a psychiatric hospital."

Ruth choked on her wine, coughing and spluttering until Lucy brought her a glass of water from the kitchen.

"I was thirteen," Anna continued, "and I was a nearly feral child. My father had left a long time before, and my mother had no idea what to do with me once I was nine or ten. My chief pastimes were glue-sniffing, vandalism, and petty theft."

"They let you out, though, in the end?" said Lucy tentatively.

"At first I was quite literally banging my head against the wall," Anna said, "but in the end it was clear that it would be easier to give in and get better than to stay there and continue to hurt myself. After that I went to a special boarding school. It was academically quite good, and for the first time I was on medication that quieted my — what is it called in English? — ADHD. I did very well there. That was the school that put me on track to where you see me today. It easily could have gone another way, though, which is why I am not sure it is really right to say the hospital was the worst thing that happened to me. My psychiatrist there, for instance, might well say that the worst thing that ever happened to me was not to be born an only child."

"Wait," Ruth said suddenly, "have I been horribly offending you with *Trapped in the Asylum*? I never thought — I'm so sorry, Anna!"

"No, no," said Anna, laughing and brushing the concern away with her hand as if it were a fly, "it is something I have made my peace with."

A ponderous silence fell, broken by Ruth's saying that she was going to bed.

"Stay and finish your drink, though, Anna," she added. "Just because I have work to do in the morning doesn't mean you two should stop hanging out."

"No, I think it's time for me to leave as well," Anna said, getting to her feet. "I ran out of coffee this morning. I'd better go downstairs to the grocery store to pick some more up, and I've got a bit of writing to do before bed. I'll just use the toilet first, if you don't mind."

"Of course not," Ruth said.

"Thank you very much for your hospitality," Anna added.

"You're very welcome."

Once Anna had let herself out and they heard the sound of the elevator arriving and its doors opening and closing, Ruth poured Lucy another glass of wine.

"I'd never have guessed Anna had that sort of background," she commented.

"Me neither," Lucy agreed. Doubt suddenly struck her. "I suppose we are quite sure she was telling the truth?"

"I don't see why someone would lie about something like that. It's the whole point of the game, isn't it, to tell the truth? She could always have turned the conversation in another direction if she hadn't wanted us to know."

"I guess so," Lucy said. "It just doesn't add up. And what did she mean when she said that thing about the misfortune of not being born an only child?"

"You should have asked her while we were still playing," Ruth said. "Then she would have had to tell you. Ask her next time you see her, though, if you really want to know."

"No," Lucy said, considering. "I don't want to be intrusive."

Ruth shrugged.

"It's your funeral," she said. "That was fun, by the way. The look on your face while Anna was on the last bit of that climb!"

Lucy went to bed feeling mysteriously and unwontedly grumpy, as though she had been accused of being a bad sport. The only thing she would ask Anna, she decided just before falling asleep, would be to stay away from high places with precipitous drops, at least while Lucy was watching.

Ruth and Lucy spent a good deal of time over the following week working in the living room on *Trapped in the Asylum*. Friday night was no exception. Indeed, the graduate student lifestyle maintained no clear distinction between weekday and weekend, a blending together of work and play that culminated, though it often let one accomplish extraordinary amounts, in the gradual erosion of the ability ever to feel free of the obligation to be working.

Ruth's phone rang around nine, and she took the call. It was her boyfriend Mark, with whom she had a strong but sometimes contentious relationship involving much debate about whether they would sleep at her place or his. He was an associate professor at the medical school, his research centered on the genetics of aging; he would preemptively observe, when people at parties wanted advice about how to avert facial wrinkles or graying hair, that the largest organism he studied was yeast. Though Lucy adhered to the polite fiction whereby one does not officially possess information gleaned from overhearing one side of someone else's telephone conversation, she gathered that Ruth was agreeing to meet Mark in twenty minutes for a burger at the Heights.

After Ruth got off the phone, she asked Lucy whether she wanted to join them, but though the invitation was extended with evident friendliness, Lucy much preferred not to. She found Mark dogmatic and overbearing on topics not directly related to his academic research.

"Lucy, you haven't seen my Guerlain lipstick, have you?" Ruth called from the bathroom.

"Is that the one that looks a little like a silver bullet?" Lucy asked.

"Yes, the one with the compact inside," said Ruth. "I could have sworn it was in my little brown makeup bag, the one on the bathroom counter."

It was most unlike Ruth to misplace something. She was careful with her possessions, much more so than Lucy, who often lost things she cared about.

"Do you remember when you last used it?" Lucy asked. "You might have left it in another bag, or even a coat pocket."

"No, that's what's so perplexing," Ruth said. "It was definitely on the counter, and I'm absolutely positive I haven't touched it since we played truth or dare. I know I was wearing it that night, and we were home all evening. There's no reason I'd have put it into my purse."

"I will keep an eye out for it," Lucy promised.

Ruth had just left when a knock came at the door. It was Anna, wondering whether Lucy wanted to go out for drinks.

"I don't feel like going downtown," Lucy said cautiously.

Her reluctance was the product of a number of factors, native frugality being one and another the implicit anxiety (about punctuality, about time wasted) that rendered the unpredictability of when the next subway train would come a source of deep irrational distress, although the recent introduction of light boards announcing wait times at her local station had partially mitigated this aspect of things.

"Walking distance," Anna promised. "We'll meet up with my friend Andrew at a bar in the neighborhood; he lives at 116th and Lenox, so it's easy enough to find a mutually acceptable spot."

Lucy had met Andrew a few times before — he was an Englishman, an architect, one of Anna's seemingly countless New York friends — and liked him well enough, except when he talked pretentiously about architecture. She cast a glance at the stack of compositions that she had intended to mark that day. Almost any other activity held more appeal and interest than grading essays; it was one of those jobs that only became bearable with the lubrication of alcohol, and a bottle of sauvignon blanc in the fridge had been earmarked for the purpose.

"You can't stay at home marking essays on a Friday night!" Anna exclaimed. "You will come, won't you?"

They walked down the stairs rather than waiting for one of the antiquated elevators. In the lobby, the night doorman told Lucy she had a package.

"I'll get it on the way back in," Lucy said, ashamed at having spent the whole day indoors and only just now crossing the threshold to the real world outside.

On the sidewalk, Anna pulled out a pack of Marlboro Lights and lit one up for herself.

Lucy checked her wallet to see whether she had enough dollars to pay for drinks and potential cab home, it having been a recent resolution not to put any drinking-related expenses on her credit card, which had an alarming lump of debt sitting on it already. She'd gotten cash the day before for a couple weeks' worth of tutoring, though, and even after having paid Ruth four hundred dollars as a prorated contribution for that month's rent (the other half would be paid in *Asylum* hours), a solid wad of bills remained. She couldn't do too much tutoring without compromising the other things she was meant to be doing (teaching, finishing the poems for her MFA thesis, writing reviews for *Bookforum* and a handful of other places), but it paid dramatically better than reviewing or teaching, thanks to the deep pockets of Manhattan private-school parents.

"So what's been keeping you out of trouble, relatively speaking?" Andrew asked Anna when they had settled themselves at a corner table in a small bar on Columbus Avenue.

"Do you know Lucy's flatmate, Ruth?" Anna said to him.

"I've met her, haven't I? She's interested in simulation and locative games?"

"That's her," Lucy said.

"Lucy and I have spent a lot of time this past month working with her on her next big project," Anna said, "a game called *Trapped in the Asylum*."

"It sounds highly Foucauldian," Andrew said. "Did you ever tour the Eastern State Penitentiary when you were in Philadelphia, Lucy?"

"Yes, I did," Lucy said. She had spent several years in Philadelphia after graduating from Penn. "It's fantastic."

"What is it?"

"You must go, Anna," Lucy said. "It's the most bizarre place, a sort of crenellated Gothic nineteenth-century fortress right in the middle of the city."

"It was built by prison reformers interested in the Benthamite model of panoptic surveillance," Andrew told Anna. "The cellblocks radiate from a central surveillance rotunda, and it was meant to be a true penitentiary. Prisoners were originally isolated and kept hooded whenever they were outside their cells, and the solitude was supposed to give them time for self-examination and repentance."

"Oh, as in the Pennsylvania system," Anna said. "Of course I know it. Lots of prisons in Europe were built along similar lines."

"Tocqueville visited the Eastern State Penitentiary in the 1830s," Andrew said, "and so did Dickens a bit later on. Parts of the movie *12 Monkeys* were filmed there."

"It's not still a functioning prison, is it?" Anna asked.

"No, it was shut down finally in the 1970s," said Andrew, "but you can still tour the buildings. It is an unusual space."

Lucy thought that this was an understatement, but then she had first gone there aged nineteen while tripping on acid with two of her closest friends from school and proceeded to have one of those unpleasantly intense experiences that makes you swear off hallucinogens forever, at least until the next time someone gives you any.

"Prisons and asylums," Anna said dreamily, her eyes closed. "Two kinds of places one would prefer to visit rather than have to live in."

*Trapped in the Asylum:* Julius Chambers' memoir had made it quite clear how difficult it might be to get back *out* of an asylum even if one's mental illness were merely feigned. Anna hadn't spoken, the night of truth or dare, of outright abuses during her adolescent hospital stint, but it was difficult not to envision a gothic milieu of sinister attendants and murderous fellow patients.

Andrew was drinking Bushmills and Anna and Lucy vodka tonics: well drinks were two for the price of one from 10 p.m. to 1 a.m., the waitress had informed them, a pricing scheme conducive to getting quite quickly drunk. What had Lucy eaten for dinner, if anything? Toast and jam in the early evening, she supposed, but nothing that would especially soak up alcohol.

Anna seemed to have been gone for a long time in the bathroom, but when Lucy said as much to Andrew, he merely observed that Anna was a person who could obtain drugs virtually anywhere and that this place put no strain on her ingenuity as at least three different people regularly sold pot and cocaine in the restrooms.

Lucy was shocked, though she strove to conceal it. It was less a puritanical alarm than a prudential one; the lawbreaker's naked vulnerability had been hammered into her as the child of immigrant parents. Outside the occasional private smoking of weed at someone else's apartment, Lucy felt the acquisition and consumption of illegal drugs presented an excessive risk.

Anna reappeared, manic and bright-eyed, and they ordered another round of drinks. Was it their fourth or their fifth? Lucy's energy began to flag, but Anna was keen to keep moving.

"I don't want to go to another bar," Lucy said helplessly.

"We don't have to," said Andrew. "I have a better idea. Have you ever been to Morningside Park at night? Truly at night, I mean, not just as dusk falls?"

"Isn't it dangerous?" Lucy asked. Morningside Park wasn't a runner's park like Central Park or Riverside Park. There was the fact of its vertiginous verticality, the cliffs and stairs that were an unavoidable consequence of the neighborhood's sharp disparities in elevation; it wasn't big enough for a real run, either, and Lucy rarely went there, though she was ashamed of herself for being slightly afraid of it. Once she'd been so immersed in a book that she missed the required change from the express to the local at 96th Street. The express train took its long sideways swerve to 110th and Lenox, and in retrospect, she should have gotten off

there and walked west on 110th before turning north up Amsterdam. Instead she stayed on until 116th, then had a frightening late-
night clamber up the flights of stairs leading through Morningside
Park to the Heights, heart racing and skin clammy with the mois-
ture of exertion and nascent panic.

Anna was unsteady on her feet as they walked north to 110th
Street and east to the park entrance at Manhattan Avenue. Andrew took one of her arms and Lucy the other, all of them ignoring
the sign telling them the park closed at 10 p.m. It was a crisp, clear
late October night, and the cliff of Manhattan schist loomed like
something out of a Gothic novel, the Cathedral of St. John the
Divine hulking balefully over them.

Lucy almost screamed when a pair of bright eyes glimmered at
her from ankle level. It was a large raccoon, greedy and feral.

"Go away!" she hissed at it, but the creature simply stared.

Anna had caught sight of it now too, and made a cooing noise to
the creature.

"Don't go near it," Andrew warned. "They're fearless, and they'll
bite if you threaten them."

"It likes me," Anna protested.

"Stay back!" Andrew said.

He chucked a branch at it. After a moment during which Lucy
thought the animal might actually launch itself at them, it turned
and slipped away into the undergrowth.

Anna was laughing.

"It wouldn't have hurt us," she said.

She flung her arms over the others' shoulders and hugged each
of them in turn. Lucy could feel her own pulse throbbing in her
neck. The adrenaline streamed through her, though they were
strolling rather than striding: it was the great paradox of New York
City's parks, this intense infusion of grooming and wilderness.

"This place is fabulous," Anna rhapsodized. "I want to come here always and only at night!"

Andrew said that he often did just that, and offered his company for future expeditions.

"There are all sorts of amazing hidden places," he said. "And it's not nearly as dangerous as people imagine."

Anna scoffed at the notion of danger.

"Now this would be the perfect place for a game," she said. They had followed the path to the park's far northern end, and stood looking out over the pond filling in the hole Columbia University had once dug as foundation of a new gym, the gym the activists of '68 stopped from being built. "The kind of anarchic game that really is why games are worth playing — don't you think so, Lucy?"

Lucy felt that she could not say anything without disloyalty to Ruth.

"Imagine that we are animal shape-shifters, and we can only take on our bestial form within the park's boundaries on moonlit nights," Anna mused. "Andrew, what sort of animal would you be?"

"A griffin," Andrew said, sounding amused. "Mythological, solid, capable of violence when roused!"

"And I am a hawk," Anna cried out. "All creatures that are natural prey fear me. I swoop down and catch them up in my claws."

"I am a coyote," Lucy said, drawn in despite herself. She shivered.

Anna was wearing boots and leggings and an oversized knee-length cashmere cardigan over her long-sleeved tunic.

"Here, Lucy," she said, struggling to get the cardigan off.

"I can't take your sweater," Lucy protested.

"I'm not cold at all," Anna said, cackling so loudly that Andrew had to shush her. "My boots keep me warm. Really, Lucy, take it!"

Lucy wrapped the sweater-coat around her shoulders and tucked her hands under opposite armpits. Her teeth were chattering.

"You're freezing, Lucy," Andrew said. "We should go."

"The topography of this area is so remarkable," Anna mused, ignoring Andrew's suggestion. "I hate it when Europeans talk about America's short shallow history. The geological sweep of time always trumps the minor accretions of human latecomers. The buildings around here might not be so old, but it seems patently obvious to me that the cathedral here as effectively secures the area against occult attack as any of the great European cathedrals can possibly do in their respective cities."

Lucy started to laugh, teeth still clattering together with cold, but Anna drunkenly carried on.

"No, Lucy, don't scoff. These true sites of force are rare, remarkable. You're used to living here, you probably don't see it, but the cathedral and Riverside Church and Grant's Tomb, they're all places of power."

"Now there's a premise for your game," Andrew commented. "Anna? Lucy's so cold, we really do have to go."

It didn't take long to walk home. It was only that the park gave you a Narnian feeling of having been elsewhere. Lucy felt warmer but sadder the longer they walked.

"Here's to the game!" Anna called after Andrew as they parted ways.

In the hallway once the elevator had let them off, Lucy tried to give Anna back her sweater, but Anna waved it off.

"I'll get it back from you tomorrow," she said. "Good night."

She gave Lucy a kiss on the mouth, with an invitation in the matter of tongue declined by Lucy. Inside, Lucy dropped her bag on the couch and went into the kitchen to get a cup of hot water to try and warm up her hands. The heat from the gas burner beneath the kettle warmed the room a little, and she felt self-conscious wearing Anna's sweater, so she took it off and draped it over a chair. Something was bumping in one of the pockets, and she felt for it to make sure Anna hadn't forgotten her keys. As her fingers closed around the object, she thought it might be a cigarette lighter, but when she pulled it out and examined it, she saw she was mistaken. It was a Guerlain lipstick identical to the one Ruth had lost.

## ANNA'S APHORISMS

### Lungs vs. gills

October 23, 2010; 5:10 a.m.

From Janet H. Murray's *Hamlet on the Holodeck* (1998):

> *Immersion* is a metaphorical term derived from the physical experience of being submerged in water. We seek the same feeling from a psychologically immersive experience that we do from a plunge in the ocean or swimming pool — the sensation of being surrounded by a completely other reality, as different as water is from air, that takes over all of our attention, our whole perceptual apparatus.

And if I were to take an offer like the one received by the Little Mermaid, transition wholly over to that new reality? Voice gone, could it be that I would find submersion in the new medium sufficient compensation for what I had lost?

*Posted in* Alternate reality, Games, Psychology of immersion

**Readergirl**     9:25a.m.
That's pretty poetic! I think of *immersion* in the context of learning

a language or reading an absorbing novel, not so much in terms of playing a game. Do gamers really use this term this way?

**ProfPacman**  9:28a.m.
Gamers may not, but academics who write about games generally do. . . .

**Anna**  9:30a.m.
I like it because it conveys something of the sensory intensity of the world of the game. Like play itself, the word immersion heightens my sense of the pressure on my skin, the temperature change and the wetness, the feeling of buoyancy.

**Ludo**  2:45p.m.
Games don't literally make you buoyant, though. (Or wet, for that matter.)

Around noon the next day Ruth knocked on Lucy's bedroom door.

Lucy was feeling intensely remorseful about the previous evening's excessive alcohol consumption; she had slept fitfully, dreaming of feral raccoons and other creatures of unspecified sinister properties living in the wilds of the park.

"Come in," she said, reaching for the bottle of water on the floor by the bed and taking a huge swallow.

Ruth had the irritatingly bright-eyed look of someone who had spent Friday night sensibly at home in bed.

"You found my lipstick!" she exclaimed.

Lucy was in no state mentally to process this statement.

"I found your lipstick?" she repeated stupidly.

"You left it for me on the kitchen counter. I have to say, I'm super glad to have it back."

"Are you sure it's yours?" Lucy asked, feeling distinctly peculiar.

"Of course it's mine!"

"But how do you know it's not someone else's, only the same as yours?" Lucy persisted.

Ruth looked at her strangely.

"It was a limited edition. I bought it a couple of years ago. Without knowing anything specific about Guerlain's product cycle, I can promise that the odds of you having happened to come across an identical lipstick in the exact shade I own myself are so diminishingly small as to amount to zero. Why, where did you find it?"

"It was in the pocket of Anna's sweater," Lucy said, feeling considerable reluctance to reveal the fact. "She loaned it to me last night when I was cold."

"It was in Anna's pocket?"

They looked at each other. Then Ruth shrugged.

"She must have picked it up by accident when she was here the other night. I'm glad to have it back, that's all."

Had it been a temptation Anna couldn't resist? Lucy felt ashamed to suspect Anna of stealing, but she knew the heady fix of lifting small objects, the sort of glow they give off and the feeling that you *have* to have them.

"Anyway, what I really came for was to see whether you want to go for a run later," Ruth said.

Lucy shuddered. She felt queasy and dehydrated, chemically poisoned. Running was inconceivable.

Ruth kept an admirably straight face.

"That bad?" she asked.

"Could be worse," Lucy said, after a quick internal survey.

"Let's go and get something to eat, then," Ruth suggested.

"It is not a bad thought," Lucy allowed. "Give me half an hour to shower and get dressed. Where do you want to go?"

"Oh, I don't care, you choose," said Ruth. "The brunch places

around here aren't that great anyway, so it's not like we'll be missing out on something exceptional if we choose the wrong one. Let's
bring our stuff and make it a working meal. I want to check in with
you on a bunch of *Trapped* stuff."

Over eggs and fried potatoes and coffee at one of the quieter
brunch places on Amsterdam, they looked at everything Ruth had
amassed. It was a beautiful little archive. The old photographs
gave a haunting sense of the pristine bucolic landscape in which
the asylum's original buildings had been set. In certain cases Ruth
had used images from other asylums of a similar period (the game's
documentation would source everything and note any historical inaccuracies), to give the feel of things like the basement dining room and the long public wards with bars over the windows.
There were balance sheets and other financial records; there were
brief accounts of the law as it concerned the regulation of asylum
inmates, including the writ of habeas corpus; there were the copies
of real historical affidavits by which physicians had consigned their
patients to the bin.

Chambers had written of the hospital's distinctive smell of chlo-
ride of lime and carbolic acid over an underlying layer of human
filth, but Ruth had regretfully concluded that it would be at present altogether beyond her technical capabilities to produce an ol-
factory module. One of the most effective things she had done, on
the other hand, was to find an actor to read out loud some of the
descriptive passages from Chambers' exposé, modified from the
first to the second person to put the player more immediately in
the game. These would be used to recreate a physical environment
that had been nearly eradicated in the intervening years.

The waitress brought the check and poured Lucy one last cup
of coffee, which she drank thirstily as Ruth packed her computer

back into her satchel in preparation for real-world reconnaissance. They walked down Amsterdam, the wind coming at them in painful biting gusts, and through the 116th Street gates towards the Broadway side of campus.

Ruth turned to Lucy, eyes bright and body poised for action with the barely contained energy of a coiled spring.

"Ready?" she asked.

"Let's do it," Lucy agreed, pride keeping her from admitting the extent to which hangover continued to predominate over the effects of breakfast.

After opening the *Asylum* app cobbled together by the developer, Ruth gave an earbud to Lucy and put the other one in her own left ear, tethering them to the iPhone after a fashion that made Lucy feel like half of a pair of conjoined twins. They faced the Broadway gates at 116th Street; Lucy glued her eyes to the small screen and watched the campus map dissolve into a photograph of the asylum grounds as they had appeared in the early 1880s.

A series of spoken directions took them up several flights of steps and across the plaza in front of Low Library to the square brick villa of Buell Hall.

"It's sort of like a Star Trek tricorder!" Lucy said, delighted despite her queasiness. It was still a struggle to walk in step with Ruth, but she had begun to get the hang of it.

Ruth kept a straight face, but her voice quavered slightly as she answered, "Yes — every girl's dream!"

Now they faced the site of the L-shaped madhouse, two stories high. Lucy closed her eyes so as to better visualize what the narrator was telling her:

The attendant at your side unlocks the front door and admits you into a hallway from whence you are ushered into a sitting

room about twenty-six feet by eighteen. Your cell is barely six
feet by nine and lacks furniture, save for an iron cot with a
straw mattress. The walls are rough-finished and whitewashed.
As you walk along the deserted hallway, the lighted gas jets
near the ceiling cast frightening shadows.

"Do you think it's worth including something about the history
of artificial lighting?" Ruth asked, pausing the narration.

Lucy opened her eyes again, annoyed.

"Artificial lighting is interesting to me, but won't it seem trivial
to those expecting revelations about madmen, abuses of power,
and so forth?"

"Maybe you're right. Just wait for a second while I make a note."

In many spots of the central quadrangle an object could be
picked up. Arriving at the location that corresponded to the central asylum building, they acquired a virtual scrap of brown butch-
er's paper and a bent pin that could be used to prick out letters in
Morse code, a secret message to be smuggled back to friends at the
newspaper. In front of what was now Butler Library, a new set of
research files became available, including information concerning
the legal status of asylum patients and accounts of how the insane
were treated in America at the end of the nineteenth century. Once
each file had been opened and read, watched, or heard through to
the end, the player got a privilege or a tool: milk and sugar for coffee, a clean set of cutlery, a pack of playing cards.

Delays in following the instructions to find the next spot or ne-
glecting to open research files incurred penalties:

You are put in a straitjacket and left in it overnight for
punishment.

"You're sure you don't want to rope in some fake attendants
with real straitjackets?" Lucy interrupted.

"Liability issues mean that's not a good idea," said Ruth.

"But the feeling of being in a straitjacket — that's something you can't really get into words."

"What happened to the whole thing of you being a poet? Aren't you supposed to believe everything is ultimately made of words? Come on, shut up, let's keep going."

An attendant drags you out onto a grated balcony. He attaches a rubber hose to a hydrant and allows the freezing water to play upon you until you are soaking and bruised.

"I still think real water would be better. Much more profoundly unpleasant, that's for sure."

"Why are you so hung up on everything being real?" Ruth sounded exasperated.

"You like real too. Real is almost always better, isn't it? Butter is more delicious than margarine, and you wouldn't rather see fake sword fighting at a Renaissance Faire than watch real fencing, would you?"

"Actually I would," said Ruth, "and I imagine a lot of other people would, too. Anyway, fencing's a completely artificial sport. It's been hundreds of years since anybody fought with swords for real."

"Maybe it wasn't the best example."

A reward achieved after reading an account of the history and etymology of the concept of asylum: you acquire an affidavit by a respected citizen proving your sanity. A reward given in exchange for correctly matching photographs of buildings with the architect's plans: safe passage to the courthouse.

Ruth was jotting down a few final thoughts on the interface, what worked and what didn't. The reproductions of nineteenth-century newspaper articles had come out a bit blurry, and it seemed that it would be wise to transcribe excerpts of this material for ease of consumption.

Lucy took out her earbud.

"Can't we go now?" she complained. "I'm freezing."

"The ideal weather for this game," Ruth said reproachfully, "will be something like seventy degrees and sunny."

On the way home, they stopped at the liquor store to buy wine. Anna was in the lobby waiting for the elevator. After an awkward pause, Ruth overheartily invited her to come upstairs for a drink. Anna said she needed to make a few phone calls but would join them shortly; she seemed oblivious to the tension, and Lucy wondered whether it hadn't really been some perfectly innocent chain of events that had led to the lipstick ending up in Anna's cardigan pocket.

Inside their apartment, Ruth asked Lucy if she would write a short blog post describing their activities that afternoon for the *Asylum* website, so Lucy sat down at the big Mac in the living room and wrote a few paragraphs while Ruth emptied the dish rack in the kitchen and cleared stacks of books off the dining table. Anna did not count exactly as a guest, and neither Lucy nor Ruth felt much compunction about having her over as a visitor to an apartment that, while it never actually descended to squalor, certainly now and again became chaotically untidy when one or more of its inhabitants was working to a short-term deadline. Ruth had higher standards than Lucy, though, and would always put out a dish of olives or a bowl of nuts if someone stopped by, or brew a fresh pot of coffee; it had more to do with some entrenched notion of decorum than an impulse actually to feed people. Lucy had intended to cook her mother's patented fried rice recipe for dinner — secret ingredient, Old Bay — but now abandoned any notion of preparing food from scratch that evening.

Anna brought a bottle of wine herself, as well as the air of bursting to share some piece of news, but another ten minutes passed before the pleasantries had been exhausted and the mine of serious conversation could be plumbed. She seemed to listen with only half an ear to Ruth's earnest report on *Asylum* progress, eating a surprisingly large number of olives and laying the stones in a row along the coffee table as Ruth enthused about the iPhone's built-in GPS capabilities and how easy it was to home in on some small subsection of map or document.

When Ruth paused for breath, Anna sat up and began to speak, her eyes shining with a visionary gleam that made Lucy slightly nervous.

"You have marked off your playground," she said. "It is a magic circle of sorts, but it's hardly very magical, is it?"

"You're not going to harp on again about haunting and possession, are you?" Ruth asked sharply. Her voice hadn't risen, but her enunciation of the words served as a warning that her temper was already halfway to being lost. "It's ridiculous, the way you only seem to think it's a proper game if it has ghosts in it. You've got an obsession with haunting, Anna. It's so infantile."

Lucy looked at her with surprise. It was very unusual for Ruth to speak so disparagingly to someone's face.

"No haunting this time," Anna said, smiling. "I will save that for my talk at the humanities center."

"You're giving a talk at the humanities center?" Ruth asked.

"Tell me when it is, Anna," Lucy said, hoping to cause a diversion, "and I'll make sure to put it in my appointment book."

"I just received the invitation. I accepted at once. Actually, I imagined I might owe you thanks, Ruth, for mentioning my name to the director?"

Ruth said nothing. Lucy thought she would have been very glad to have been able to take credit for the invitation, but that she had probably not in this case been its facilitator. Was it that Ruth felt threatened by Anna's encroachment on a field of human activity, namely gaming, that Ruth considered her own peculiar preserve? Or was Ruth merely angry because she thought Anna had stolen her lipstick?

"I don't have the exact date yet," Anna added, "but it will be in mid-December sometime."

"Are you really going to talk about ghosts?" Lucy asked, because a silly question was preferable to an awkward silence.

"Not ghosts as such, but I'll lay out a few case studies that interest me and perhaps talk about intersections between hauntology, urban archeology, and gaming. I am truly curious about the pervasive nature of the metaphor of haunting in so many of these games. I really owe you thanks regardless, Ruth, for prompting me to take some of these questions up again. I haven't thought so much about games since I moved from Stockholm to Copenhagen five years ago."

"In that case, you're very welcome," Ruth said coldly.

"I'm going to go back downstairs and see if the mail's here yet," Lucy said, hoping a temporary alteration in the room's configuration of human personnel would discharge some of the tension. The post hadn't yet been delivered when they came in just then; it was a perennial point of complaint in the building, the tendency of delivery time to drift ever later in the afternoon. Lucy was expecting a check for her *Poetry* review of a collection of villanelles composed by a former pastry chef, and had been scrutinizing the mail anxiously all week. "Anna, do you want me to look in your mailbox as well?"

"No, thanks," Anna said. "I get my mail at the post office; I don't use the box here."

"That seems unnecessary!" Ruth said. "Isn't it inconvenient to have to stop by the post office to collect your mail? I've avoided the post office on 112th Street like the plague ever since I realized I could send letters and packages from the UPS store on 115th Street instead. It's ridiculous how much better the service is there."

Anna shrugged.

"You make it sound like a great deal of trouble," she said, "but really it's nothing."

"What made you decide to set it up that way?" Lucy asked.

"I prefer not to give out my physical address if I can help it," Anna said. "It's a question of privacy, and of safety: I don't like the thought that someone who wants to find me could actually show up on my doorstep in person without warning."

Lucy thought this sounded slightly paranoid, but Ruth was nodding.

"Yes, my high school friend Rachel had a problem with a stalker," she said. "Once you have a crazy person obsessed with you, you basically have to be incredibly careful for a long time afterward. That means keeping really tight control over who even has your phone number, let alone your street address."

"That's partly why I'm not on Facebook," Anna added.

"All right, then, I'll be back in a minute," Lucy said, picking up her keys and leaving for the downstairs mail run. The review check still wasn't there, alas; it was the usual dreck of flyers, a utility bill in Ruth's name, alumni magazines, charity solicitations, and offers for magazine and theater subscriptions. She tipped most of it straight into the recycling bin beneath the mailboxes and went back upstairs.

She found Anna and Ruth in the middle of what seemed to be an intense conversation about Anna's early history. Lucy wished she'd been there to hear the beginning; as it was, Anna was just saying that not long after she herself had gone into the psychiatric hospital, her brother had been put into foster care.

"You have a brother?" Lucy asked.

"His name is Anders, and he lives in Stockholm," Anna said. "I would say that he was not so lucky as I when it came to surviving our childhood unscathed, though I suppose it is also a matter of making one's own luck. He doesn't talk much about what happened to him in care, but mostly it wasn't good."

"What does he do now?" asked Ruth. It was the inveterate New York question; Ruth, too, was ambitious, accomplished, in just the ways such New York questioners tend to be.

"He designs sets for plays, and sometimes he directs them also," Anna said.

"Oh, so everything really did turn out all right for him," Ruth said confidently.

Anna smiled, her eyes shadow-hooded by the beam of the lamp beside her. Suddenly and fancifully, Lucy felt that darkness to be the shadow of the hospital, or perhaps just of Anna's troubled adolescence: it was a melodramatic way of thinking about someone one actually knew, but then life seemed to fall more often into the patterns of melodrama than ideally mandated by the aesthetic proprieties of tasteful storytelling.

"In many respects, we both turned out better than anyone could rightly have expected," Anna added.

"Do you and he look much alike?" Ruth asked.

"Very much alike. He is a year and a half older, but when we were younger, people often thought that we were twins. He is taller, but you would easily spot the resemblance."

"A brother — it is something I wish I had," Ruth said, musing.

"Yes, a brother," Lucy agreed. "I never wished I had a sister, but having a brother always seemed as though it must be the best thing in the world."

It would have been reasonable to deduce from Anna's expression that she found both Americans criminally naive.

"Ruth, I haven't yet told you about my idea for a game," Anna said, possibly eager to change the subject.

"You want to design a game?" Ruth asked skeptically. "I know it's an academic interest of yours, but that doesn't mean you're equipped to make one yourself. I must have created half-a-dozen smaller ones before I made my big species die-off games in graduate school."

Lucy knew that these games had been called *Amphibian Amnesty* and *Honeybee Haven* respectively, and that Ruth ranked them second in her oeuvre only to her PhD thesis project, a text-based adventure called *Lazaretto!*

Anna ignored Ruth's territorialism.

"It's a game set in Morningside Heights," she said, "but one without any of the technical elements you're using for the asylum game — no handheld devices, no programming. A simple game of urban exploration with a fantastical web-based storytelling component."

"Is that the game you started talking about last night in the park?" Lucy asked.

Ruth turned to stare at her.

"What park were you in last night?" she asked sharply.

"Morningside," Anna said dreamily. "It was beautiful. . . ."

"You shouldn't go there at night!" Ruth said.

"It was perfectly safe," said Lucy defensively, though Ruth was really only echoing her own thoughts.

"Wasn't it freezing?"

"It was a little cold, in the end," said Lucy, "but it was nice for a while. Oh, Anna, let me get your sweater for you while I think of it. Thanks again for lending it to me."

"You're very welcome," Anna said pleasantly. There was nothing in her manner to suggest anything odd about the transaction, and Lucy decided that it couldn't be that she'd stolen the lipstick on purpose. If Ruth didn't say anything, Lucy certainly wouldn't bring it up.

"It must have been late that you were out," Ruth commented. "You were still just hanging out here doing nothing in particular when I left at ten. Did you walk over there together later on?"

"First we had drinks with Anna's friend Andrew," Lucy said.

"You did?" Ruth said slowly. "You should have called me, I would have come with you."

"You had just gone to meet Mark."

Ruth's eyes followed Lucy and Anna's exchange of glances, and Lucy felt the field of alliances in the room shift, Lucy somehow thrown into partnership with Anna, Ruth positioned against them.

Anna continued to eat olives, resting her feet on the coffee table with an air of divine ease. Lucy felt a small surge of pleasure at the elegant lines of her body. Anna wore a pair of black tailored trousers that were at once perfectly plain and sublimely well cut. Her neatly shaped ankles were bare, her narrow feet clad in an odd pair of soft leather shoes with seams and minimal soles that managed to look at once functional and startlingly stylish. Ruth could have told her what brand they were and how much they might have cost; Lucy only knew they exuded luxury.

"It will be a game of make-believe, like the ones we all played as children," Anna told Ruth, who irritably poured herself a second glass of wine and snatched up a fistful of chips. "The built environment of Morningside Heights will play a more prominent role than it would in a straight fantasy."

"Do you imagine you'll serve as game master yourself?" Ruth asked, her voice ostentatiously neutral but the turn of phrase latently disparaging.

"Oh, yes," said Anna, "though I reserve the right to play as well. I am envisioning a very simple game. There's some setting up to do in advance, including the web stuff, but it will be largely self-sustaining once it gets going. It will be great fun, I hope, at least for those willing to enter fully into the spirit of play. I want it to build to a spectacular culmination — I almost said *conflagration!*"

Someone who loved games as much as Ruth did could not resist this sort of teaser. "What's the basic premise, then?" she asked grudgingly.

"Morningside Heights is a magical realm," Anna said, "a sacred conclave defended by properties laid down in the actual buildings themselves by the architects who designed the neighborhood a hundred years ago, figures like Frederick Law Olmsted and McKim, Mead, and White. Men whose occult powers remain hidden from conventional historians of architecture but whose achievements in those realms have long been marked in counterhistories of the city. . . ."

Ruth was listening closely.

"McKim, Mead, and White built many of the most powerful

and privileged edifices in New York City," Anna continued. "Madison Square Garden, the Harvard Club, and the Century Club, the arch in Washington Square Park, the Morgan Library, and the old Penn Station, whose razing to the ground in 1963 presaged many of the city's gravest troubles. Olmsted is of course most famous for Central Park, but Riverside Drive and Morningside Park were two of his best-judged sallies in the battle against the forces of evil. After the massive bloodshed of the Civil War, both Olmsted himself and the triumvirate of McKim, Mead, and White — at least until White was shot dead at a nightclub for having an affair with another man's wife — had to create a bulwark of protection to shield residents of the city from demonic onslaughts. Right down to the present day, outside forces continue to attempt to erode the magical boundaries that surround the neighborhood — "

"Are those forces players, or merely a set of constraints built into the game?"

"Not players, but the game master will monitor a series of assaults on the integrity of specific buildings that will be affected by the actions of players within the game."

"What do players have as their goals?"

"Each player initially operates individually. The invitation to the game comes by way of a rabbit hole. The players are recruited on the Internet by word of mouth for a game that is described in provocative but general terms, and at that point they are asked to sign a waiver and give all of their contact details, but several weeks pass before the real invitation is issued, and players won't necessarily recognize it when they first see it. It's triggered when the total number of players reaches a preset number — fifteen, perhaps, or even twenty."

"How exactly will the invitation work?" Lucy asked. She knew the term *rabbit hole:* it was what game designers called any kind of clue that took players into the world of the game without explicitly announcing itself as such; the invitation might be disguised as a telephone marketing survey or a website on which some piece of the world of the game actually represented itself as reality.

"Wouldn't you rather be surprised?"

In fact Lucy did not enjoy being surprised, and had the habit of looking to the end of the book she was reading to see what was going to happen, but Anna clearly had no intention of divulging more, no matter how deeply Ruth might probe.

"Wait and see," was all she would say.

**Subject:** [NYC Urban Exploration] Grant's Tomb and environs
**From:** AlleyPally <all . . . @gmail.com>
**Date:** 11/6/2010 1:18 AM
**To:** *nycurbanexploration@googlegroups.com* (cross posted at LTV Board, Max Access Facebook private group, New Amsterdam Archeologies forum)
Hey, everyone! I'm worried about my friend Cuchulain. He's been checking out locations in Morningside Heights, and he had a couple of near misses where the cops almost caught him. Last I heard, he was planning an after-hours visit to Grant's Tomb, but he hasn't posted on his blog for several weeks now. I've texted him and left a ton of voicemails, but his mailbox is full and it doesn't seem like he's checking messages. I'm starting to wonder whether he might have seen something that got him into trouble. His blog has a pretty full record of where he went in the couple weeks before he went off the grid. I was hoping some of you guys might take a look and let me know where you think he might have run into danger. I've set up a private group for discussion; ping me if you want me to add you there. AlleyPally

**Subject:** Re: [NYC Urban Exploration] Grant's Tomb and environs
**From:** BridgesnTunnels <jas . . . @yahoo.com>
**Date:** 11/6/2010 1:21 AM
Sure. I go up there a lot; will write you off-list if I hear anything.


**Subject:** Re: Re: [NYC Urban Exploration] Grant's Tomb and environs
**From:** NinjaNineteen <nin . . . @yahoo.com>
**Date:** 11/6/2010 1:23 AM
AlleyPally's kidding herself—friend C. just ditched her for another ho.


**Subject:** Re: Re: Re: [NYC Urban Exploration] Grant's Tomb and environs
**From:** EnduranceGirl <sha . . . @gmail.com>
**Date:** 11/6/2010 5:20 AM
Ninja, your misogyny is not appreciated.


**Subject:** Re: Re: Re: Re: [NYC Urban Exploration] Grant's Tomb and environs
**From:** BBB <bui . . . @hotmail.com>
**Date:** 11/6/2010 8:03 AM
More bluntly, Ninja's an asshole!


## EXCERPTED FROM CUCHULAIN'S LIVEJOURNAL

---

. . . it's pretty clear to me now. The century-old protections built into some of the critical buildings of Morningside Heights have eroded. It's partly due to neglect, but I'm beginning to suspect that it's also a question of malicious attack. There's a very real possibility that some kind of sorcerer is systematically dissolving each one of the protections placed at tactical places around the neighborhood's borders.

The fire at St. John the Divine was the first sign that something was deeply wrong. I remember that morning very well: it was December 2001, a few days previous to the winter solstice, and the early-morning sound of helicopters in the air above Morningside Heights as I walked to the Hungarian Pastry Shop told me that the balance of powers had toppled out of its proper equilibrium.

The cathedral retained its structural integrity after the fire, but the aesthetic and spiritual damage was incalculable. Several of the stained glass windows actually shattered, though the firefighters were tender of the building's fabric and left as much as they could intact. Repairing the damage would take literally years, with parts of the building closed off from worshipers and the restriction of prayer further degrading the neighborhood's wards.

It's nothing out of the ordinary to think of buildings serving to anchor or ward entire areas: the influence of the Flatiron Building fans out over a fifteen-block radius within which both people and property are strongly buffered against psychic attacks. Statues can do this sort of work too: Pushkin's tale of the equestrian statue of Peter the Great coming to life may be the most famous literary instance, but everyone who knows anything at all about New York knows that the Statue of Liberty, the stone lions in front of the Public Library, and the crouching cougar on Cat Hill in Central Park are all doing their bit to protect the city.

Morningside Heights has its own team of statues, providing an essential extra layer of ritual protection. Statesman and reformer Carl Schurz stands over Morningside Park, and politician and philanthropist Samuel Tilden is stationed near the Hungarian patriot Lajos Kossuth on Riverside Drive south of Grant's Tomb.

But each month seems to bring new episodes of vandalism and defacement. To the high-minded slogan on the plinth of Tilden's statue — "I trust the people" — was appended the cynical graffito "No you don't": nothing much in itself, of course, but taken cumulatively, all the protective powers that came by way of these figures stationed around the perimeter of the Heights were being chipped away, siphoned off. I came to see that if that process wasn't halted and reversed, we would be increasingly open to the attacks of demons and other entities too dreadful to be imagined.

"A team of urban explorers is needed to walk the boundaries of the neighborhood," Anna said, "and reinscribe the ritual protection that will prevent an evil sorcerer from being able ever again to threaten the safety of someone like Cuchulain."

"Architecture and the occult — that's so *Ghostbusters,*" Ruth said. If Lucy hadn't known how much Ruth loved the movie, she would have thought the observation entirely dismissive.

"Walk the boundaries in a literal sense?" Lucy asked hastily.

"Yes and no. The act of walking along the required lines is certainly part of it, but the neighborhood will need to be woven back and forth with protection. Protection needs to be documented and recorded on a map online, and players will mark a trail of protection around individual buildings as well as limning the bounds of Morningside Heights as a whole."

Ever since Lucy had first read *The Lion, the Witch and the Wardrobe* at age six, she had been unable to resist the notion of proximate alternate worlds into which one might, if one were peculiarly lucky, be able to walk without any conscious intention to cross over. She had no vested interest in games, only the ordinary suburban American child's history with them (jacks, Candy Land,

Twister, spin the bottle), though it struck her as strange that even someone so uninterested in games as she considered herself to be should have spent so many hours playing them (Monopoly!).

"Have you put the map up already?" Ruth asked.

"No, not yet, but I was hoping you might come out with me now for a little reconnaissance to do with what instructions I might give to the players about how they will enact the rituals of protection," Anna said, her voice shy rather than brash, the words addressed to Ruth. "I would greatly value your help."

Ruth couldn't resist the appeal to her own authority.

"Let's go, then," she said, standing up and going to the coatrack by the door. "Lucy, are you coming?"

"Yes, I think so," Lucy said. "Where shall we go?"

They walked over to Riverside Drive and turned towards Sakura Park, a small quiet enclave directly across the street from Grant's Tomb, which Lucy passed by regularly but had never entered. Just past the park was another one of those steep drop-offs that gave the neighborhood its sense of self-containment. It was nearly dark, the trees bare of leaves.

"John D. Rockefeller was the original owner of the land," Anna announced. "It was he who paid for the park's landscaping."

They stood in one of the avenues lined with linden trees, trees whose branches would join in spring to form a sort of canopy over-head. Between the two linden walks was a bare lawn with a pretty gazebo and a huge number of cherry trees, nothing special to look at in winter but resplendent in spring; the trees had been donated by New York's Japanese residents a hundred years earlier, and the park served as host every spring for a cherry festival. A statue of the Civil War general Daniel Adams Butterfield, composer of the bu-gle call "Taps," stood at the back of the park facing Grant's Tomb to the west.

"The avenues, the gazebo, the lamp," Anna continued, "which one do you think would provide the most convincing repository of energy?"

Lucy left the other two and began pacing along the avenue.

"The gazebo has to figure into it!" she called back to them. "Players might draw some sort of pattern along the paths, with the gazebo at the center?"

"You can't encourage people to deface public property," Ruth said repressively.

"No," Anna said, "but if they use something like chalk or a scent bag of the sort that hunters use to mark a trail for dogs to follow, that wouldn't hurt, would it?"

"I like the idea of the scent bag," Lucy said. "It reminds me of a children's book called *The Wind on the Moon*. The two girls in the book get a very smelly bag from a witch called Mrs. Grimble, and she tells them to use it to mark out a protective circle at least a hundred yards wide around the house where their friend the golden puma needs protection. When men with dogs come after the golden puma because of the farm animals she had killed, the dogs just run around and around the circle the girls marked on the ground without being able to break inside it."

"How long do you think it would take, then, to drag a protective figure along all of the park's paths?" Ruth asked.

"It's not a big park," Lucy said, "but the crisscrossing will add up, won't it? You don't want to give people a job that will take forever."

"We'll walk it and get an estimate," Anna said crisply.

They walked the paths together, Lucy using the stopwatch function on her Timex to make the calculations. The traces of a hop-scotch square could be discerned on one open spot near the back of the park, the ghostly scrawl uncannily speaking to the recent physical presence of actual children. Lucy saw something bright on the ground and leaned over to pick it up; it was the thick nub of chalk used to draw the square.

"Look!" she said. "We can trace the circle so that it is actually visible to others!"

"Very good," said Anna, though in fact it was prohibitively uncomfortable to crouch low enough to the ground to drag the chalk along while also moving forward. Lucy drew about twenty feet of line before giving up and leaving the task to some more fit and flexible future person.

"Two other places of power can be found nearby," Anna announced when they had finished walking the perimeter. "I'm talking about Grant's Tomb and Riverside Church, where Martin Luther King Jr.'s speech once sealed protective wards tightly but whose protections have begun to erode."

"Let's go and look at them another day," said Lucy. Her feet were cold and she wanted another drink. "I need to pee. We should go back to the apartment."

"The question is how to instill meaning in the act of drawing a chalk line on the ground," Anna said, once they had shed layers and kicked off shoes and used the bathroom and poured themselves more wine and resumed their former positions: Lucy as usual sitting by the dining table with Ruth's big computer as a kind of shield between herself and the others, Ruth with pink cheeks from the cold and looking suddenly rather beautiful, Anna with the compact sinuous grace of a reticulated python.

"It should feel like a ritual, not like a child's street game," Ruth observed.

"It can't be just any old chalk," Lucy said, not quite sure what she meant but feeling strongly the justice of the words. "It has to be *special* chalk!"

"Yes, special chalk," Anna reflected. "Perhaps the chalk itself must be won in some earlier stage of the game?"

"I guess so," Ruth said, "but if you want everyone to acquire a piece of it, you're going to have to be very clever not to make the whole thing seem a setup."

"The chalk needs to be set into some kind of a holder," Lucy said, thinking out loud. "It will be difficult to imbue chalk on its own with that magical feel, but if it is set into some little bullet-shaped holder that sits nice and snug in the palm of the hand — "

The thought of the purloined lipstick was strongly present to her.

"I know the sort of thing you're imagining," Anna chimed in. "Let's say something made of black lacquer with gold symbols painted on it?"

"Yes, something small and compact and beautiful, those are the lines I was thinking along," Lucy said.

"It's a lot of work to make high-quality props," Ruth warned.

"Napkin rings!" Lucy said. "That's what I'm thinking of — a napkin ring with some kind of a block to wedge the chalk into place inside the ring, or a thick enough piece of chalk that you can jam it in securely on its own. Just using ordinary chalk on its own won't do anything — the chalk has to be paired with the device!"

"You can go to the dollar store and see what you can find," Ruth suggested.

"The *dollar store?*" Anna asked.

"A fairly horrible sort of shop where almost everything costs ninety-nine cents," Lucy glossed.

"You need to be careful, or the costs will mount up exponentially," Ruth said sternly.

Anna and Lucy caught each other's eyes, and Lucy had to fight not to be overwhelmed by mirth. Ruth so perfectly embodied, sometimes, the puritanical virtues of American life, that it was ironic that her chosen specialty should be games. Even the games Ruth created were corseted by the strictness, the asceticism of her own imagination. Her attraction to the dollar store was utilitarian, and invited some of the same implicit irony as her love for games: how could somebody with that keen a sense of purity and beauty, of the inbuilt intrinsic quality of things, be drawn to the sorts of cheap awful trinkets obtainable at the dollar store and its ilk?

The living room in which they were sitting, for instance, was sparely but beautifully furnished, with a few pieces of classic American mid-century design in the way of furniture (more beautiful to look at than comfortable to sit on), an oatmeal-colored Berber carpet and a set of shelves mounted above the sofa to display Ruth's eclectic collection of roosters. Ruth only owned things that were perfectly beautiful and functional, from the vintage Fiestaware pottery in the kitchen cabinets to the Stuart Weitzman shoes sitting in a neat row on the floor of her closet. Lucy had only ever had a fake Prada bag, bought for ten dollars on Canal Street one day when the strap of her tote bag had broken nearby under the weight of too many books, but Ruth had a real one. A Montblanc fountain pen lay atop the unusual cloudy polyurethane blotter on the brushed-steel drafting table Ruth used as a desk. Even the collection of Ruth's material possessions was regularly and ruthlessly pruned, with worn or otherwise extraneous things going to the donation center at the parish house of St. John the Divine. The line of suits and dresses that hung in her closet had the edited quality of a boutique, with none of the messy overstuffed bargain-basement feel of a normal person's closet.

"New York is a strange place for someone who has mostly lived in the Scandinavian countries," Anna said. "Some things are very expensive here, which is quite familiar to the inhabitant of Stockholm or Copenhagen, but then some things are so very cheap!"

"Not everything is expensive in Stockholm," Lucy objected. "When I was there the summer after college, I hardly had any money at all, and I loved the way you could always get a hot dog on the street outside a club, even at five in the morning. A delicious hot dog, too, not like the ones the vendors sell here, which are boiled forever in disgusting vats of smelly water."

"Drinks are quite cheap in this neighborhood, though," Anna observed. "In Sweden, everyone I know drinks at home first before going out, so that they need only buy one drink at the club rather than three or four. It is much more economical that way. But though I see that you two do sometimes drink at home before going out, my intuition is that this is because you are students — "

"I'm not a student!" Ruth protested.

"Well, in student-like stations in life," Anna amended. "It is not a general practice in New York, is it, to drink extensively at home before going out to a bar or a club?"

Lucy giggled helplessly. "Anna, that's such a sociologist's question!"

"It is not a general practice in New York to drink a great deal at home before going out," Ruth agreed, more good-humored than before.

"You two do not seem to take drugs at home either," Anna continued. "Is this more generally true of Columbia students and faculty, or would you say that this is anomalous?"

Now Lucy and Ruth were both laughing outright.

"Some do, some don't," Lucy said, taking a gulp of wine and coughing as it went down the wrong way. "But you should know, Anna, if you're interested, that the way most of my New York friends buy drugs is by home delivery."

"Home delivery?" Anna asked.

"You call your dealer, and he sends a minion to bring you what you have requested and collect the money," Lucy explained.

"Interesting," Anna said. "Does the minion come in a car?"

"To the best of my knowledge, the deliverymen — and let's not use the ridiculous term *minion,* it's so inappropriate! — rely on public transportation," Ruth explained. "Buses, perhaps, these days, now that they're so often searching bags at subway entrances, and then of course there are always bicycles."

"My friend Daniel would give you a phone number," Lucy commented.

"I don't think it would be wise for Anna to purchase drugs while she's in this country on a student visa," Ruth said primly.

Anna shrugged.

"American attitudes towards drugs seem far more repressive than European ones," she said. "I had heard as much, but I did not realize the extent to which it would be borne out by my experiences in New York."

## ANNA'S APHORISMS

### Momentum

November 15, 2010; 1:09 a.m.

The game called *Momentum* (2006) lasted for five weeks without interruption of any kind. Continuous play was enabled in part by the ingenious decision to ask players to play two roles: each player was both "herself" and "herself as possessed by the spirit of a dead revolutionary." The particular revolutionary to possess each individual was assigned by the game master (given identities included murdered Marxist revolutionary Rosa Luxemburg and government-executed Nigerian activist Ken Saro-Wiwa), and the game was played continuously for thirty-six days with no interruption.

Players were asked to play the game as if it were real.

The game included thirty players; its designers rented out a defunct nuclear reactor hall underneath Stockholm and used it as an underground headquarters which featured a war room, lounges, meeting rooms, a control room, and a gym. There was also a so-called ritual hall, which was fitted with paranormal technology the players were trained to use during game play. *Momentum* culminated in a massive public demonstration in which the revolutionaries were exorcised, allowing them to return home on All Hallow's Eve. A safe word was provided, so that characters could step out of game as needed, but it was used only a handful of times over the course of the game; players would participate actively in the game for a few hours each day during the week, and then all weekend from Friday evening to Sunday. Some players actually moved to the headquarters for much of the duration of the game.

*Places of Power* asks for a similarly round-the-clock commitment from its players, though we do not have a physical headquarters to offer. Open your senses, though, to the feeling of being threatened from outside and the need to shore up New York City's defenses. Morningside Heights is vulnerable. Do everything you can to protect it.

*Posted in* Games, Ghosts, Invitations, Places of Power, Possession

• • •

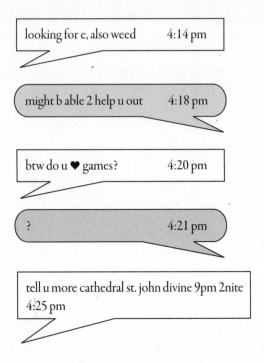

looking for e, also weed     4:14 pm

might b able 2 help u out     4:18 pm

btw do u ♥ games?     4:20 pm

?     4:21 pm

tell u more cathedral st. john divine 9pm 2nite
4:25 pm

Ruth had dinner plans and Anna was meeting a friend at nine, so Lucy ended up spending the evening lying on the couch reading a battered mass-market paperback copy of Aldous Huxley's *The Doors of Perception,* purchased for two dollars from one of the vendors on Broadway. She fell asleep around eleven and woke feeling surprisingly well-rested. Consulting the clock on the kitchen wall and then the schedule stuck to the refrigerator with a magnet in the shape of a white chess queen, she saw that she would have plenty of time to make it to her preferred Sunday-morning yoga class. After eating a piece of whole-wheat toast with grapefruit marmalade, she went back into her bedroom and dug the appropriate garb out of the hamper of unfolded clean clothes that seemed a permanent adjunct to having laundry only in the basement.

Though the air was chilly and crisp, the sun warmed her as she walked down Amsterdam and then along 106th Street to Broadway. Class was sparsely attended this morning, which was all to the good; Lucy didn't enjoy the feeling of being thronged about on all sides with people more flexible and limber than herself. This was a fast-paced and athletically strenuous vinyasa session taught by a woman called Maggie who moved about the room quietly adjusting students' alignment without leaving one with the feeling of having been decimated by critique.

Yoga had been an eye-opener to Lucy. She avoided dancing and more generally thought of the body as something strictly functional; one had to have one, and it was to be hoped it wouldn't let one down, but it was hardly likely to be a thing of beauty or even a particular focus of attention. Lucy lived in a world made up largely of words and ideas, and was happy enough that it should be so. But the premise of yoga was quite different. Here, molding one's body into the proper configuration was the only way to understand the idea of the pose. You had to have the right position of the sacrum and pelvic bone to get tree pose, say; you had to make sure that the front hip was really properly rotated and the femur aligned horizontally before you would really get any glimpse of the underlying notion of warrior two. Yoga could not be done just in the head; it had to be done in the body as well, and the shapes that the body went into couldn't be explained in words. You only understood them when the teacher tugged a knee in one direction or pressed down along your back, and then suddenly you felt at least for a moment what the pose really was in its essence. These traditions had to be transmitted from person to person; they could not be described and summarized in a book, though one might use a line drawing or a YouTube video to refresh one's memory of a pose or get some approximate sense of proper form. But the true pattern of meaning could only be expressed in a body; it could only be passed from one body to another.

Resting in corpse pose at the end of class, eyes closed, a blanket draped over her by the teacher, Lucy found her mind had gone almost blank. It was with regret that she perceived the lights had been turned back on. It was time to go. She lay there for a moment more before rolling onto her side and pushing herself up for the final *namaste*. Putting the props away (she always took a couple of blocks and a belt to ease the poses requiring a hamstring flexibility she did not naturally possess), and folding her blanket and stacking it back on the pile, she went to retrieve her shoes and bag and jacket from the side of the room where everyone left things.

She was the last one; there were no shoes left beyond her own scuffed matte black clogs. But someone had left a notebook on the floor. Lucy couldn't decide whether or not to leave it there for whoever had forgotten it or take it up to the front desk. She decided on the latter, as another class would begin in fifteen minutes. Picking it up, she surreptitiously leafed through; there was no name at the front, but the book was full of richly colored and slightly manic sketches of eyes and faces and bodies, a claustrophobic glimpse into a densely imagined and overfigured hallucinatory world. She dropped it at the front desk with an explanation of where she had found it, the girl there thanked her, and she went out into the street, drawing her jacket more tightly around her when the wind cut through her clothes.

That would be one way of inviting someone to play a game, it occurred to her as she wandered up Broadway in the direction of home: an orphan notebook, carefully situated, with something in it so intriguing and urgent that nobody who came across it could leave it where it was.

She bought half-a-dozen bagels (poppy, whole wheat, salt) and some scallion cream cheese at Absolute, then stopped at the Greenmarket by the Columbia campus for apples, a quart of pear cider, and a jar of sour cherry–apricot jam. It was the most delicious confiture she had ever tasted, to the extent that she couldn't always stop herself from eating it with a spoon straight out of the jar, and only the lack of a utensil prevented her from unscrewing the lid right then and there on Broadway and consuming a delicious mouthful. Pear cider, too, had an agreeably magical air to it, conjuring up a land in which orchard fruit and its byproducts were the conduit to a green world like Narnia or Kipling's Pook's Hill.

Back at the apartment, Ruth had taken over the kitchen for what would be only the first of many forays in her massive annual cookie-making undertaking. It was long-standing Ruthian tradition, as it had been her mother's and grandmother's before her, to undertake true Christmas cookie present-giving, and baking thus began in mid-November, a week or two before Thanksgiving, with cookies that could be frozen without sacrifice of flavor and freshness, the predetermined order of cookie-baking set by an elaborate rota that had been developed by the women of her family over many decades.

Lucy sat at the kitchen table and tinkered with lines of a conjectural poem.

> "Dot-and-carry-one," name for a gait. Dot an
> archeological remnant, too, of the naming practice
> belonging to an older generation. The letter D, dash-dot-dot.
>
> Gait analysis, artifact
> of the age of film. Running-store remedy

for shoe woes. Gait.
And then the vicissitudes of foot placement:
asphalt, concrete, tarmac, grass, dirt.

She became distracted by the question of which Elizabeth Bishop poem used the word *tarmacadam*. And was it tar-MAC-a-dam, rhythmically congruent with *lorazepam,* or tar-mac-AD-am, given that Wikipedia told her (a short trip to the computer to check her email had led her down a winding set of detours) the word referred to a road construction method invented by a Scot called John Loudon McAdam circa 1820?

The Internet did not make it easier to write poetry. It was cheering, though, to think of the end of the semester being so close: there was a mere week and a half of classes before Thanksgiving, and only two full weeks of school after that. Of course, that didn't do justice to the amount of grading and the sheer volume of student meetings to be dealt with between now and winter break, but after having taught the first-year writing class a couple of times already, Lucy found it relatively manageable. It occurred to her that she should set up a meeting before the end of the semester with the advisor of her MFA thesis, who became elusive out of term-time just as Lucy's own schedule tended to open up.

She persuaded Ruth to stop rolling out dough for long enough to join her over a bagel and coffee. Cookie-making was a ritual more frazzle-inducing than calming, and Ruth seemed even more tightly wound than usual. Lucy felt remorseful when she contemplated the slight distance that seemed to have emerged between them over the preceding weeks. It was impossible to put it down to a single cause. Her slight irrational dislike of Ruth's boyfriend? The disparity between Ruth's schedule and Lucy's? Ruth was always up very early in the morning, whereas Lucy found it difficult to get out of bed before eleven or so, and always taught in the afternoon or early evening so that she would have time before class to prepare that day's lesson plan and finish the inevitable backlog of grading.

Whatever it was, something had tipped them noticeably off kilter, and it might even have been their mutual unwillingness to discuss the question of whether Anna was to be trusted. Though it was possible that Ruth and Lucy actually spent more time officially socializing together since Anna had moved in next door — if socializing was the right word — and though initially the threesome had been inseparable, Anna's presence itself since the affair of the lipstick had come to work on Ruth as a kind of irritant. Around Anna, Ruth seemed more humorless, less warm than she did otherwise — and this despite the fact that Ruth had become engaged enough in Anna's *Places of Power* that she had taken to running the bounds of Morningside Heights every other morning, as though the rhythm of her feet touching the ground and the ring she drew around the border might have magical force. Ruth started and ended her run at Grant's Tomb; Anna had more than halfway convinced both of them that the Civil War must have represented a massive occult conflict, with the snowball effect of death on such a massive scale raising thousands of demons, small ones at first and then greater ones in their wake. Grant gave his life to fight those demons, Anna insisted, and it was no coincidence that so many of the figures memorialized in the statues of Morningside Heights were wartime generals: these were the men whose training and temperaments had put them on the front lines of battle with the forces of darkness.

Lucy contemplated Ruth's face with regret; it was in its beautiful rather than its plain aspect just now, flushed from the heat of the oven, but she almost wished Ruth wouldn't say anything and would just allow herself to be gazed upon.

The phone on the wall in the kitchen began to ring, taking them both by surprise. It wasn't a number either Ruth or Lucy gave out readily, both of them using their cell phones for pretty much everything, but Ruth kept the landline and an old-fashioned non-electric phone as a precaution in case of emergency. In the days after 9/11, it had been nearly impossible to put through a cell phone call, and also there had been the strange antediluvian interlude of the blackout that wiped out the electricity supply of the whole northeastern United States in the summer of 2003, during which it had become clear that a telephone that worked when plugged into the jack but with no other power source was an instrument one might find it worth one's while to retain.

"I'll get it," Ruth said, setting down a bit of bagel and dabbing her lips neatly with a napkin.

Lucy's phone was turned off. Tuning out Ruth's side of the conversation in the kitchen, she turned her own phone on and saw four voicemails.

When had she last had it on? Probably not since early afternoon Saturday, she realized, though surely anybody sensible would send an email to find her rather than trusting to voicemail or text messaging.

"Lucy?" Ruth was saying, leaning through the kitchen doorway with a worried expression on her face. "It's for you."

And in the next few minutes, the rest of Lucy's semester changed catastrophically. It was a doctor calling from the hospital in Lower Merion where Lucy's mother had been admitted the previous evening after a serious car crash. Her left femur and hip were essentially shattered, and she had broken a number of other bones; they were worried about the implications of a head injury whose extent couldn't yet be assessed. An initial surgery had been performed to stabilize her, but extensive further surgery would be needed in the coming weeks to repair the damage.

"There are a lot of unknowns," the doctor said, her voice kind, weary, a touch impatient. "It really will be best if you can get here as soon as possible."

Lucy scribbled down the hospital's name and a few different phone numbers on the back of a ConEd envelope. She hung up the phone and put her hands over her eyes. There was so much to do! Rent a car, for a start: she usually took the train to Philadelphia and her mother picked her up at the station, but that wouldn't work now, and it was impossible to get around in the suburbs without a car — and what about her classes?

Ruth had already comprehended the essentials and was turning on the computer in the living room. "Just tell me what you need," she said firmly, guiding Lucy to the couch and making her sit down, then bringing her the half-finished mug of coffee from the table. "I can book a car for you really easily with Hertz. If you pack quickly and take a taxi to pick it up at 96th Street, you'll be on the road in an hour. You can text your tutoring students to cancel. What about your classes for this week?"

"Annabelle will cover for me if I ask her," Lucy said dumbly. "I taught a couple for her near the beginning of the semester when she had stomach flu, and her class syllabus is very similar to mine. In fact, we're workshopping paper drafts both days this week, and it won't take much time for me to get her up to speed."

"Do you want me to send her an email explaining, and tell her that you'll call her later?"

"Yes, that sounds right," said Lucy. She couldn't think at all clearly.

"Let me plug in your phone and make sure it's fully charged," Ruth said briskly. Her no-nonsense willingness to take Lucy in hand was an immense relief. "Your laptop's working, isn't it? You'll definitely want your computer with you, in case you need to be away for longer than you think."

Lucy's heart quailed at the thought of what awaited her — even a couple days seemed like an intolerably long time to be away — but it was true, she should bring enough stuff that it wouldn't be super-penitential to be stuck out there in suburban Philadelphia for a number of days. The bag she packed, she later realized, contained the most impractical mix of things: a toothbrush but no tooth-paste or deodorant, and more books than anything else — a biog-raphy of Randall Jarrell, a manual for the Total Immersion swim method, poetry collections by Siân Hughes and Terrance Hayes, and, presciently or just preemptively, an anthology of poems about grief and loss.

In the end, Lucy barely got back to New York in time for the start of the second semester. During the intervening weeks, things had begun to happen: things that would change everything.

## II

# PLACES OF POWER

GENERAL GRANT AND HIS WIFE, on adjacent tombs, were positively Brobdingnagian in scale. When Anna darted around the other side of the basement rotunda, I walked after her, trying not to betray my anxiety about being left behind in this eerie Civil War mausoleum. I was relieved but perplexed when I found her kneeling on the floor, her left ear pressed to the side of one enormous sarcophagus.

"What are you doing?" I asked.

She put her finger to her lips. "Listen!"

Feeling like a complete idiot, I kneeled down and placed my own ear to the stone beside her. I couldn't tell if it were simply some kind of auditory hallucination — perhaps I was hearing the beating of my own heart — but it was almost as though Grant's life force still pulsed through the containing walls.

"Ruth?" Anna whispered.

"What?"

"What do you think it would take to wake the dead?"

I snorted and rocked back on my heels to look at her directly.

"I'll give you that this place is eminently suitable for designation as one of your places of power," I told her, "but I wish you wouldn't talk as though it really would be within our capabilities to bring General Grant back to life."

"Who's to say it's not? No, Ruth, don't be angry, I'm not joking—"

She hurried after me as I strode up the stairs to the main level and made for the exit.

"You'll still come tonight, won't you?" she cajoled.

"I told you, I always meant to watch the eclipse with Mark, and I don't want to break a promise."

"You'll regret it if you don't come."

I stopped and turned back so that I could see her face.

"That sounds almost like a threat," I said flippantly.

Anna wasn't wrong, though. I might complain, but something in my hard little soul (it was Lucy who had bestowed this unflattering moniker on my immaterial substance) had melted towards Anna's game. Her talk at the humanities center late the previous week had been electrifying; attendance was low due to the time of year, but all those present had been engaged and captivated by what she had to say about Nordic live-action role-playing, and a few attendees had even been lured into participating as players in *Places of Power*. I wouldn't have been entirely sorry had Anna shown herself to be a poor public speaker, but nonetheless I found myself longing to help restore the places of power to their original potency.

Over dinner later that evening with Mark (I had defrosted some of the pesto I'd made that summer from the basil we grew on his balcony in pots, serving it with linguine alongside a simple green salad), he and I fell into heated argument.

"I know I said I'd watch the eclipse with you from the roof of your building," I said, "but this is a once-in-a-lifetime opportunity."

"Watching it with me is a once-in-a-lifetime opportunity too," Mark said, with uncharacteristic petulance.

"It's the coincidence of the full lunar eclipse with the winter solstice that's so unusual," I said patiently. "It's the first time it's happened in probably five hundred years, and Anna's game is uniquely tailored to highlight the conjunction. In fact, I'm tempted to go out on a limb here and say that really, you're the one who should be coming with me, not the other way around."

Mark looked at me like I was crazy.

"I think it's the stupidest thing I've ever heard," he said bluntly. "Not to mention you might get arrested."

"Oh, didn't I tell you? Anna decided it was too risky to try for either of the roofs, Grant's Tomb or St. John the Divine. We're just going to meet on the cathedral grounds."

"I guess that's moderately less idiotic than the original plan, but I still think it's pretty stupid," Mark said. "Don't you remember that guy getting himself arrested on the cathedral roof not long after 9/11? The SWAT officers and the antiterrorism squad didn't really care to hear his assertions as to the nonthreatening nature of urban exploration. . . ."

"Nothing like that's going to happen tonight," I said in my most soothing voice (I am a good girlfriend, really). "We'll only be in the grounds, not inside the building itself, and the eclipse makes for a good cover story if anyone tries to stop us."

"Obviously I can't prevent you from going. I can see you're absolutely set on it. But I don't want any part of it myself."

Anna's celestial observances didn't begin until two in the morning, and after cleaning up the dinner things, I lay down next to Mark in bed and put my arms around him. He rolled away from me, though, and when I looked inside myself, after half an hour of tossing and turning, I found that I didn't actually feel very kindly towards him, either.

"Are you asleep?" I asked softly.

He didn't answer, so I got up and dressed and crept out of his apartment and made my way home.

It was a chilly damp night when I walked over to the meeting point. (Chilly but not truly cold, not for December in New York.) A few of the others wore balaclavas to hide their features, but most of us just had on ordinary coats and hats and gloves. Clouds masked the part of the sky that interested us, but we had opened a gate into the cathedral grounds and found a quiet little corner with a clear line of sight to where the moon was supposed to be.

Just then the clouds spread enough for us to see the phenomenon we had all been awaiting: the moon's white orb cast into shadow as the earth moved between moon and sun. We began to walk in a circle, widdershins, all of us keeping our faces turned up to the sky like a little belt of miniature moons. As we tromped out our ring, the real moon emerged again from behind the shadow, white no longer but rather a baleful red.

"Stop!" Anna called out.

We stopped dead in our tracks. Our hands were linked in one large circle; Anna had made it very clear beforehand that breaking the circle would release all the power we intended to accumulate by way of the ritual, and it would mean failure if that happened too soon.

"Kiss the person on either side of you to seal the circle," she commanded.

It sounded vaguely unhygienic to me, and I couldn't bring my-self to give the young man to my left anything more than a brief, brisk smack of lips on cheek. Others took the injunction more se-riously and actually exchanged saliva.

Anna herself stood inside the circle without being of it.

"I need a partner for the next piece," she said quietly; we had to crane forward to hear her. "A partner without fear, someone whose purity of heart and intention will provide the energy needed to reseal the broken portal of St. John the Divine and raise again the protections built of old to armor Morningside Heights against oc-cult depredations."

Two or three people seemed to want to step forward, but the one who tugged most forcefully and speakingly against the bounds of the circle was a beautiful boy with chestnut dreadlocks, probably in his early twenties and with an athlete's rather than an intellec-tual's physique. I thought he might be one of half-a-dozen bike messengers who had responded to Anna's initial shaking-out of players from the urban exploration woodwork via message boards and flyers.

Anna came over to him, gave him a chaste kiss on the forehead, and then a warmer one on the mouth. He tried to lift his right hand to touch her face, and she slapped him once, hard, on the cheek.

"It is my sole prerogative to unseal you from the circle," she said in a remote manner. "Wait for my hand on yours, and for my join-ing together of the hands of those on either side of you. You must stay bound until I say the word."

She dropped to her knees and unfastened his pants.

(What on earth did she intend to do now? I was suddenly very glad Mark hadn't come with me after all.)

"I will swallow your seed, and kiss the ground with your seed on my lips. Then you will spill my blood over it on the earth, and we will thereby reestablish the ritual protections."

I could not say whether the rest of us were more aghast or mesmerized. Only the force of Anna's personality held us there. She went on to give the boy a dramatically authentic blow job. Our solstice celebration seemed to me to have crossed the bounds of legality now, even aside from the question of trespassing. I just prayed (that's an idiom, not a literal use of the verb!) that the police wouldn't arrive and ask us what we were doing. This sort of development could only lead to all manner of mess, including perhaps permanent consequences in terms of an arrest record: the sort of thing I preferred to avoid, given my not-yet-fully-fledged academic career.

The boy was moaning now, and as we watched, his hips began to jerk. Anna rose up from in front of him, lips sealed tight, then threw herself prone on the ground in the center of the circle. She kissed the stone beneath her, opening her lips to leave a smear of semen on the ground, then stood and claimed the boy from the circle, making sure before she tugged him after her that the hands to either side of him had been properly joined one with another.

"You must all chant quietly as we fulfill the last part of the ritual," she told us. "Just say 'St. John the Divine and Morningside, St. John the Divine and Morningside.'"

"St. John the Divine and Morningside," we said obediently after her. "St. John the Divine and Morningside."

She whispered something into the boy's ear. He looked briefly balky, as though he were inclined to turn her down, but she leaned up and said something else to him that made him shrug and follow her to the center of the circle. It was hard to see what happened next; it all went by so quickly. Over us the red orb of the moon was undergoing the last part of its transfiguration. But what I thought I saw was Anna putting her hand to the boy's and drawing it to her breast. With her other hand, she pulled open the layers of coat and sweater and shirt she had donned against the night's damp chill. Then she pulled his hand hard and quickly along her collarbone down into the cleavage. Blood welled up in a drippy line along the trajectory.

"What did she just do?" the girl to my left whispered to me.

"I couldn't say," I whispered back, wishing she hadn't broken my immersion. Was it a stage effect, or had Anna drawn a hidden blade along her own skin and released real blood? I was nearly certain it was the latter.

I became even more sure it was so when she rubbed her fingers in the red stuff and kneeled down on the earth in the same place as before, pressing her hand to the ground. Next she stood and touched her chest again and dabbed her bloody fingers on the boy's forehead to make a sort of Ash Wednesday smudge. His own hand went to his face, and he looked slightly grossed out and maybe even a little scared when the red came off on his fingers.

Anna began to move around the circle, touching her hand to her chest (it looked like a gesture of humility, though I guessed her feelings were more on the order of triumph) and then letting her fingers briefly rest on each person's forehead, marking us with her blood.

"Three more times for the chant," she commanded.

"St. John the Divine and Morningside! St. John the Divine and Morningside! St. John the Divine and Morningside!"

"Now throw your hands in the air and look up at the moon and howl. The boundaries of the Heights have been resealed. Let the night revels begin!"

I didn't join them at the bar on Amsterdam Avenue. I went

home unsettled but also (I hated to admit it) a little excited by what I had witnessed. In bed I tossed and turned restlessly until I faced the fact of my arousal; then I masturbated until I found relief.

I slept for a few hours, but woke up again around eight. I got up, put on a kettle, and found myself very much regretting Lucy's continued absence. I felt sorry for Lucy, but I also felt sorry for myself. Lucy was an excellent roommate, barring occasional slight untidiness (but I knew myself well enough to know that I preferred to be the tidier rather than the less tidy member of a two-person household, with the slight self-righteous burn of washing someone else's dishes now and again being infinitely preferable to the feeling of having someone else breathing down my neck in the matter of putting things away). I liked the modest additional income stream that came from having a roommate, but I also liked the emotional stability I derived by dint of having someone else almost always around, in which regard Lucy was truly perfect: she preferred home to every other place, and the hours in which she was not actually teaching or acquiring reading materials at the library or perhaps exercising were hours in which she was at my disposal as researcher and sounding board. It was true that I found her habit of obsessing about a single word or a line of poetry annoying, but in general, it had to be said that I missed her a good deal.

I cuddled up on the couch with a quilt and a mug of mint tea, but as the clock ticked its way towards nine (I use the term *ticked* metaphorically, of course; I am acutely sensitive to noise, and though I have a real clock on the wall in the kitchen, having been thoroughly indoctrinated by my mother into the notion of an analog clock forming a necessary part of any kitchen's decorative scheme, all other clocks in the apartment are digital), I acknowledged that I didn't quite know what to do with myself this morning. Baking would have been an acceptable fallback possibility, but I had finished my holiday baking the week before and parceled out the decorative tins to their designated recipients; indeed, the stress of holiday baking was partly accountable for my current tightly wound state. Purposeless baking was something I could not bring myself to do, as I avoid eating sweets myself and Lucy was no longer in residence to sample whatever came out of the oven.

I heard some activity down the hall. It felt undignified and a little stalkery, but I peeked out to see if it was Anna. She was standing in front of her door and fumbling with the keys; I called out a hello to her.

"Ruth!" she said, turning to me with her key still in the lock. She looked terrible, I thought: pale and drawn, eyes red-rimmed and clothes in disarray.

"Are you all right?" I asked.

She shrugged and opened the door. "Come and have a cup of tea with me before I go to bed. When I was in my teens and twenties, I could stay up all night without it bothering me, but I can't say that's any longer the case."

I sat at the kitchen table while she put on the kettle and placed tea bags in mugs.

"Do you mind if I take a quick shower?" she said. "I feel filthy, even if it's mostly just the effect of staying out all night drinking and smoking marijuana."

"No, go for it." When the kettle boiled, I poured water into the mugs and took mine to the living room, leafing through a couple of fashion magazines and wondering afresh how Anna could possibly afford the clothes she wore.

Anna reemerged post-shower in a dressing gown, hair turbaned up in a towel, and draped herself along the other end of the couch.

I fetched her mug from the kitchen (it was chamomile, soothing for the digestion), but as I leaned over to put it on the coffee table, I was alarmed and appalled to see the deep gouge along her neckline, the edges already puffing up and splitting open like the slash in the crust of a baked Brie.

"Anna!" I said, slopping the tea on the table. "You cut yourself very badly last night!"

She looked at me quietly, reaching for the tea and taking a sip before putting it on the coaster.

"The blood was needed," she said calmly, "to complete the ritual."

"It's a fucking *game,* Anna! You don't have to stick a knife into yourself and spill your own actual blood. You're an idiot. That's going to leave a permanent scar. Don't you think people will wonder about it? Potential employers, or maybe people you might want to go out with? You're going to come off like a total wack job."

Anna shook her head obstinately.

"I don't care what people think," she said. "It wouldn't have been the same if I'd used theatrical special effects. The earth knows. . . ."

Suddenly suspicious, I scrutinized her pupils, but they were no more dilated than normal. It seemed likely to be pure unadulterated crazy rather than drugs. This, I felt, was a pity. The altered state of drug use is usually temporary. Genuine crazy tends to run considerably deeper.

Feeling distinctly unsettled by the thought that Anna might really be something of a lunatic, I said finally, "Let me clean the cut for you at least."

"I already rinsed it off in the shower."

"I've got peroxide and tape and gauze down the hall. It looks pretty nasty, and you don't want it to get infected."

Anna did not actually refuse to submit to my ministrations, so I dashed back to my apartment and raided the medicine cabinet for supplies. I was only gone for a few minutes, but when I got back, I found her asleep on the couch. She barely cracked open the lids of her eyes as I began to clean the deep V-shaped cut that started at the top of her collarbone and plunged down a few inches over one breast and back up along the contour of the other one. Close up, I could see that it sliced through a tangle of raised scars, some pale and barely perceptible to eye or finger and others more deeply ridged and still red around the edges. Anna was a longtime cutter.

I found a duvet to cover her with and left her to sleep. Back at home, I brewed a fresh pot of coffee and read the news online. I couldn't seem to settle down to any kind of real work, and if I'm honest, I'll say that it really wasn't so much that I was short on sleep or worried about Anna as that I was waiting for Mark to call and apologize for not coming with me to watch the eclipse at the Cathedral. I didn't know how well he would have liked the spectacle, but as a matter of principle, I felt he should have been willing to make my priorities his own.

I was determined that he should be the one to call, not me. I was in the habit of sleeping over at his apartment approximately three times as often as he stayed at mine; he said that this made sense, as his bed was more comfortable and he didn't have a roommate, but I had come to suspect the ratio might be indicative of some more fundamental imbalance in our relationship.

We were not spending Christmas together; he was flying on the twenty-fifth to California to stay for a week with his brother and sister-in-law and their two young children, while I would go as I always did to my mother's for the Christmas Day festivities. I had casually suggested that Mark might come with me to her place for the holiday — we had been dating for more than six months now, and I was fairly certain the relationship had a future — but he hadn't taken the hint.

The hours went by. I refreshed my Google Reader continuously, but everything got stupidly quiet around this time of year. The only things online were best-of-year roundups, endless top ten gift lists and recipes for things I had no desire whatsoever to cook or eat. I got an email from my friend Anya at the humanities center that had in its subject line only an exclamation point; inside the message was a link. When I clicked on it, it took me to a post on Bwog, the blog of the Columbia undergraduate literary magazine called *The Blue and White*. It was about me! Or, rather, about my game:

> **Trapped in the Asylum?**
> Whether you're a first-year or a senior, you know the feeling of being trapped in a madhouse (Butler 24-hour study rooms, anyone?). But if you're still reeling from finals and don't go home for another couple of days, check out this crazy new game. Your hardy investigator heard about it from a fall-semester TA, and enlisted a couple of people to play with her. (You need your own smartphone, but if you don't have one of those by now, you are so thoroughly doomed to a life of misery and complete social exclusion that not being able to play this game will be the least of your worries.) Download your mission instructions from the game's website, then start at Buell Hall, and walk through a day in the life of a real nineteenth-century madman. Bonus points for whacking your mother to death with an axe or poisoning your sister with arsenic — and once you get a look at the food asylum inmates were given in those days, you'll never complain again about the meal plan at John Jay.

The link to my site was broken, and I dithered about whether or not it would be appropriate to leave a comment. Finally I decided that it would (it wasn't like I was criticizing what they said about me—I was just making sure that others could find the site!). There were five additional comments by now, two from trolls but the others sounding genuinely excited about playing *Trapped in the Asylum*. I basked in the momentary unexpected glow; indeed, it gave me enough of a boost that I could finally face wrapping my mother's present.

My mother was difficult to shop for, as she essentially sacked the treasure shelves of Bergdorf and Bloomingdale's every week without regard to cost, but she also collected nineteenth-century American children's toys, and though I had to be careful not to duplicate items already in her collection (the one I found would always be in some inconspicuous but definite way inferior to the one she already possessed), I had this year discovered a very lovely hand-carved pig, its paint somewhat faded and chipped but otherwise in excellent condition, that I knew she would find suitable.

Mark still hadn't called, and gradually the lift of the *Trapped* publicity dissipated. Finally, he texted me around eleven thirty (a call would have been more appropriate!) to suggest that we meet for dinner at Max Soha at seven. I texted him back to concur. Texting is not a medium to express complex feelings, but I could see that perhaps it was wise not to be transmitting a toxic fog of irritation and mild holiday-precipitated distress by way of live phone conversation.

I spent the afternoon in my office at the humanities center. Most of the other fellows seemed already to have departed for their respective holiday peregrinations, and I annoyed myself by eating several quite inferior holiday cookies I discovered on an already heavily pillaged tray in the staff kitchen. Since I'd been dating Mark, I'd gained almost five pounds; clearly the consequence of eating hamburgers and drinking beer with him at the Heights (one of his favorite local eating spots, despite the intolerably loud music and a marked tendency to attract drunk undergraduates), and as one of my goals for the intersession period was to lose those pounds again, cookie-eating was distinctly counterproductive. If I were going to eat a cookie, I could at least eat a delicious one, not one of these stale color-sugar-sprinkled mediocrities!

In short, I found myself incapable of dispelling or even merely disentangling the mixture of feelings that afflicted me. Could it just be grumpiness that my own life lacked the near-psychotic intensity Anna brought to so much of what she did? Was I having a metaphysical post–*Places of Power* hangover?

A new Anna's Aphorisms entry had come up in my Google Reader. I had often wondered whether Anna knew or cared that I read her blog. She never alluded to it, and neither did I, almost as though it were a facial birthmark we had politely agreed not to mention.

## ANNA'S APHORISMS

### All of the above

December 22, 2010; 1:52 p.m.

The logic of sacrifice: I give up something valuable for — what? The reinvigoration of the earth? The good of the group? The transfiguration of the self? I would even give up my life if the promised return were sufficient.

*Posted in* Death, Sacrifice, Tradeoffs

I felt more uneasy than I had before, and resolved to keep a close eye on her over the holidays.

Around three I realized I was getting nothing done. There was no point staying any longer. I went home and unpacked my work things. The depressing atmosphere at the humanities center probably meant I had better avoid the place until after the holidays. There was no point putting in face time if nobody of any significance were there to register my presence; all the fellows knew that the powers that be *did* note who was always there and who was absent, and although there were no further goods as such to be distributed, it was felt, at least by myself and a few others, that one might as well keep on the good side of those who administered the Society of Fellows. Some of the other fellows might resent my pragmatism, but we all knew that being in or out of favor affected crucial matters such as office allocation (space at Columbia was perennially tight), extra funding for outside speakers or conferences, and so forth.

I changed into my running clothes, putting on an extra layer and making sure that I had my gloves and ear warmers as well as the usual long tights and thick socks, and ran over to Riverside Drive and down into the park. Lucy almost always commented when we ran down this wide avenue of trees together that it reminded her of a children's fantasy novel, as though one might just vanish off the end of the path into some alternate reality; I found this annoyingly whimsical and was not sure why she felt the need to say it so often (I had after all heard the observation perfectly clearly the first time!), but the thought made me miss her.

It was almost dark. Barring a few other runners and a handful of people walking dogs, the park was virtually empty. I decided not to run through the tunnel down to the Hudson, instead turning around at the playground north of 96th Street and running back along Riverside Drive with its steep hill (the elevation gain was quite marked). I was breathing heavily by the time the ground leveled out at 106th Street, and I jogged the rest of the way home feeling calmer than I had all day.

I pulled down the blinds so that I could strip off my damp clothes and put them in the hamper, then took a luxuriously hot shower. I dressed in my favorite pair of jeans and a charcoal gray cashmere V-neck sweater to which I affixed the Jensen silver rooster brooch given to me by my mother for my eighteenth birthday.

I was ready a bit too early, an occupational hazard for the compulsively punctual, so I gave the kitchen a quick clean, thus making myself slightly late. The restaurant was only moments away, and I considered and then dismissed the possibility that Mark had chosen it in a mute gesture of apology, since he knew I preferred the food there to the Heights. It was significantly closer to my apartment than to his, and I wondered whether he could be persuaded to stay over at my place tonight, notwithstanding his complaints about the size of the bed (double versus queen) and the overly firm mattress. His flight didn't depart until early afternoon the next day, and I believed he didn't intend to go in to the lab in the morning, so there was no reason he shouldn't stay over.

In fact it was 6:57 when I walked in the door at Max Soha, and I had after all arrived punctually in advance of Mark. The hostess seated me right away; it wasn't too crowded, since much of the usual Columbia clientele had already departed for the holidays. I took out my phone and texted a couple of gaming friends who had promised to do a dry run of *Trapped* over the winter break.

Wasn't it a problem, though, that I couldn't offer them anything like the drama of Anna with the blood rolling down her breasts? I have never been exactly sure how I came to be so obsessed with games. People who meet me at parties often seem surprised that a person who studies games should appear so self-contained and humorless. I usually counter this observation by saying that games are a serious business. Most players of games are very much in earnest, not so much frisking and frolicking as furthering their interests like rational actors in any other field. Games represent a field apart, that is all, not a field distinctly different in its priorities from any other. I say all of this in a relatively dry manner that leaves the person I am talking to quite unclear whether I mean to be funny or not.

(I am in fact a person with a sense of humor.)

Mark was usually quite punctual himself, but it was almost 7:20 by the time he finally arrived. He slipped into the seat opposite me and unwrapped his scarf, then struggled out of his coat. Seating was tight and it was a good thing nobody was sitting at the table next to us. The waitress came by and he ordered a glass of merlot; I suggested that we get a carafe. I had already drunk most of a large bottle of sparkling water by myself.

"No, let's just get individual glasses," said Mark. "I have to go pretty soon. You know my flight leaves tomorrow, and I haven't packed yet."

I looked at him with surprise. It was quite common for us to split a carafe of wine, at least if we were at the sort of place where one drank wine as opposed to beer, and I had imagined that we would at the very least spend a lazy companionable evening together. I had his present back at the apartment, and I was hoping he'd gotten me something too, though I was ready to take it philosophically if he had not. (It will sound annoying of me, but having been raised by a supreme present giver in the person of my mother, I much preferred to receive no present at all rather than get an ill-chosen or unattractive one.)

"Ruth, there's something I've been meaning to tell you. . . ."

Now I just stared.

"Mark, are you breaking up with me?"

He looked singularly sheepish.

"I'm sorry, I know it's bad timing, but I've been meaning to say for a while now that I thought the time was coming when we should call things off. I thought you'd understood what I meant when I told you I couldn't come to your mother's for the holiday, but then it seemed as though you were assuming we'd go on as we have been. I've enjoyed spending this time with you, Ruth, but I don't see it working out in the long haul, do you? It will be better for both of us if we cut things off now before either of us gets too deeply involved."

"You're breaking up with me!"

He couldn't refute it. He was definitely breaking up with me.

I was surprised to find tears welling up in my eyes. The waitress arrived just then with our glasses of wine, but as she put them down, I was already assembling my things and struggling back into my jacket.

"We just broke up, I won't be staying," I found myself saying to her.

"You're sure you don't want to stay for a drink at least?" Mark asked, looking a bit relieved.

"That's all right," I said.

"Take care," he called after me as I made my way to the door.

I wasn't thinking anything at all as I rushed home, other than very much hoping nobody I knew would see me crying in the street. The evening doorman had stepped out to do his security rounds, and I fumbled for my keys for what seemed like forever before someone came up behind me and said, "Here, let me get that."

She unlocked the door and held it open for me, then said, "Ruth! Are you all right?"

It was Anna. I looked at her closely, but she seemed buoyant, energized, not at all depressed or suicidal. I swear that if you'd seen her that morning, you'd have thought she was permanently broken. Now she gleamed and glowed again, her presence bursting with life and energy, and I felt pallid and uninteresting by comparison. Anna: Anna whose game, improvised in a matter of weeks, might well have outdone any game I'd ever made, even though I considered game design my life's work; Anna who brought out all my competitive instincts; Anna whom I found attractive and repellent in equal measure. Anna who was about the last person in the world I wanted to see me bawling in the lobby of my apartment building a few days before Christmas!

She must have known that if she drew me into her arms, I would have bristled and recoiled, for she did no such thing, just put a hand to my shoulder and steered me towards the elevator.

"You will tell me about it over a drink," she said. "I have just the thing."

"Just the thing for a broken heart?" I said bitterly.

She turned to look at me as we stepped into the elevator, her mouth twisting into a wry expression, and I started laughing despite myself.

"I know, I know, it's not that bad," I said, snuffling grotesquely.

"It may be fairly bad, but I am guessing it is eminently survivable," she said. The doors opened and she pushed me along straight to her apartment.

She had spent at least part of the day cleaning. The floors were glossy, everything looked spotless, the air was redolent of Murphy's Oil Soap and Lemon Pledge. I cannot explain how it happened (the consumption of significant quantities of horseradish-infused vodka may have been a contributing factor), but an hour later I had told Anna a great deal: not just about Mark and how devastated I felt by the end of our relationship and my dread of what my mother would say when I told her, but also my lurking fear that the remnants of eating-disordered behavior (an adolescence spent battling anorexia, an ongoing and in fact recently resurgent practice of binging and purging) meant that I would never have a permanent life partner.

The quality of Anna's attention was exceptional. She sat next to me and held my hand and patted it, all the while gazing at me with her face open to mine as a face might open up to bright sunlight. She soaked me up like a sponge. I had been off and on either suspicious or envious of her for months now, and the *Places of Power* game had in certain key respects only heightened that negative affective orientation. But seeing Anna as vulnerable rather than powerful had changed my feelings towards her, and I resolved to put aside my negativity. True, Anna might be a kleptomaniac and a cutter, but then as a graduate of one of Manhattan's finest and most prestigious girls' schools, I knew that mild-to-moderate kleptomania and self-harm were at least as prevalent in the female population of elite educational institutions as eating disorders, and after all, who was I to throw the first stone? She was a good listener: she seemed to have near-infinite patience for my moaning, hardly saying a word herself.

"Anna, what are you doing on Christmas Day?" I asked. I had begun to feel slightly queasy, the effect no doubt of neat liquor on an empty stomach after a run, but I focused on settling my stomach and keeping my eyes focused.

"I will see Swedish friends on Christmas Eve," she said. "In Sweden, as you may know, we chiefly celebrate the holiday on the twenty-fourth."

"You'll come with me to my mother's for Christmas dinner, then," I resolved. I ignored the small voice in my brain that was saying *You want to take this crazy melodramatic self-harming madwoman to your* mother's *house?*

"I would be honored to accompany you," said Anna, her language as always quite formal and impeccably grammatical.

"I think I had better go and lie down," I said.

"Yes, do that, Ruth," said Anna. "I cannot say that you will feel better in the morning; in fact I am certain you will have a hangover, but I have enjoyed our talk. What time do we go to your mother's?"

"We might get a cab from here around one on Christmas Day; the main meal is usually served at three thirty or four in the afternoon."

"Very well, then. I will knock on your door just before one."

As I let myself back in to my own apartment, I remembered that I had turned off my phone when Mark arrived at the restaurant, and it suddenly occurred to me that he might have called to tell me it was all a mistake, he'd changed his mind, he really did want to be with me after all and had canceled his trip to California and would come with me to my mother's instead. But when I turned it on again, there were no messages. The surge of distress I felt then was so acute that it drove me to the kitchen, where I pigged out on a disgusting quantity of food (at least five ounces of cheddar, an entire bag of SunChips, a sleeve of shortbread and three sugar-free chocolate puddings), at which point I went to the bathroom and stuck my finger down my throat. Of course it might mitigate some of the next day's inevitable alcohol hangover, but I already felt the shame I always associated with purging, and made a resolution that come the first of January, I would swear off binging and purging for once and for all.

Lucy would certainly rather have been in New York if she could and in any case it was not her fault that I got so crazy about my weight, but I depended quite a bit on Lucy's presence to make myself feel tolerably adequate about my own size and eating habits. Lucy wasn't exactly fat, but neither did she have the slender build often associated with Asian American women. She had broad shoulders and a sturdy square torso, muscular but with some extra padding, and at 5'4" or so she probably weighed around 150 pounds. The number I saw on the scale myself usually sat around 115, though it was hovering dangerously close these days to 120, which seemed to me an absolutely unacceptable numerical transition. (I am only 5'3".) Anna was extremely slim — I would have been surprised if she weighed more than 110 — and exactly my own height; standing next to her made me feel like a cow.

The last straw came when I saw my present for Mark sitting forlorn on the coffee table. It was a brushed-metal card case, as he was in the habit of handing out dog-eared business cards from the back pocket of his jeans; I had found it in a museum store several months earlier and wrapped the box in a colorful but masculine maroon paper with a discreet forest green bow. Impulsively I tore the present open and took it out of the box and into the kitchen, where I placed it on the cutting board and banged it with the meat-tenderizing mallet until it fell apart in pieces. Then I went to bed and cried myself to sleep.

I felt predictably awful the next morning. I cleaned up the mess of Mark's present and drank a couple glasses of water. Then I went for an hour's run and weighed myself afterwards; 117, even with the benefit of what was probably fairly major dehydration. After I'd showered and changed, I threw out almost all of the food in the fridge and the cupboards, then made a seriously healthy shopping trip to Fairway, resolutely turning my eyes away from the cheese section (cheese was my vice) and buying chicken breast, a piece of tuna, eight ounces (two servings) of beef filet, and a huge quantity of vegetables: spinach, broccoli, radishes, sweet potatoes, carrots with their tufts of greenery. (Lucy would probably have mentioned Peter Rabbit, as she did, too, whenever I drank chamomile tea.) Fruit would be too much of a temptation, and there would already be more than enough temptation at my mother's place, as well as copious reproach from her to me regardless of whether I indulged or stinted myself.

Mark still hadn't called, and at that point I decided that he wouldn't. (I was still hoping he would, but I said to myself that he wouldn't so that I couldn't be disappointed.) I would have liked to be very busy, but in fact, though a great deal of work remained to be done in terms of logistics for the next iteration of *Trapped in the Asylum,* nobody was answering my phone calls or emails, and I grudgingly had to allow as how the holidays made it nearly impossible to get anything done.

The Columbia gym was closed as well, but if I ran for more than three days in a row I would be courting shin splints, and having a spell without any running at all really *would* make me crazy, so instead I put down a yoga mat on the living room floor and did Jillian Michaels' *30 Day Shred* until my muscles trembled with fatigue. It was a gloomy day, chilly and a little damp; the weather this whole month had been unseasonably cold and unpleasant, though I liked the way it meant the running paths in the park were so much less crowded. On Christmas Eve I huddled on the couch and watched episodes of *Firefly* for about the fifty millionth time (it was my great comfort to imagine myself as a member of that alternative family congregated as crew on a rogue spaceship far from Earth). I was starving, but the fridge and kitchen cupboards now only contained the sort of food that wouldn't trigger a binge, which also meant there was nothing I felt like eating. I drank some miso soup and fell asleep under the quilt on the couch, the TV still on.

On Christmas morning I woke up early and had a nice run in Riverside Park. I went all the way down to the sanitation pier at 59th Street; there weren't many other runners out, and we exchanged smiles and nods as we passed one another, happy in the secret shared knowledge of there being no better way to start a holiday than with a run. It was chilly but sunny while I was out, though the clouds had begun to make it feel cold again as I came out of the park at 116th Street, running up the steep final bit of hill on the path to the park exit as hard as I could. I walked the rest of the way home, picking up a cup of coffee and a cinnamon-raisin bagel at the store en route. Exercise usually quieted my hunger, at least temporarily, but I was for some reason ravenous this morning; at a stoplight, I put down my coffee for a moment on one of the free-newspaper dispensers, stuck my hand into the greaseproof bag, and tore off a chunk of bagel and stuffed it into my mouth.

It tasted incredibly good as I swallowed, but it seemed to lodge like a lump of clay in my esophagus. Disgusted with myself, I threw the rest of the bagel away in the trash can at the next corner.

As I waited for the elevator in the lobby of my building, I resolved that I would eat exactly as a normal person would today, neither under- nor overindulging, in an attempt not to attract my mother's attention to my eating. I weighed myself in the bathroom (I hadn't had more than a couple sips of my coffee) and the scale said 116; I resolved that I would be down to 112 for sure by the end of the calendar year, and that I would exercise every single day from now on for as long as I could.

(My longest streak of this sort in prior years had been 163 days, but I thought it would be perfectly realistic to shoot for 365. Walking didn't count; it had to be something where you either went to a class or otherwise really worked up a sweat, but Jillian Michaels was fair game, and once Lucy was back I would go with her to yoga or get her to run with me on a regular basis. She was a slow but very steady runner; she did a half marathon now and again, and though I was rather faster than she was, if we were just going out for three miles or so, a six- or eight-mile run would find Lucy just as strong and steady as ever in mile seven even as I myself flagged and fought the temptation to walk.)

I had showered as soon as I'd finished my coffee, then dressed again in pajamas and dressing gown. I wanted to wear something nice to my mother's, but it was chilly and damp enough outside that the thought of going back out filled me with reluctance amounting almost to dread. I tried on several different pairs of pants, and was relieved to find them fitting right again; I settled on a favorite pair of black slacks from agnès b. and a red cashmere sweater I'd gotten the previous spring on sale at Tse.

I was ready a little too early. I took my shearling coat off again (slimline leather gloves tucked into the pockets), turned back on my computer, and wrote Mark an email wishing him a merry Christmas (it seemed less personal than texting, and also less pitifully requiring or requesting a response), sent it, and then immediately felt absolutely awful. I was such an idiot sometimes, I reflected, and went into Lucy's room and rummaged through the drawers of her bedside table until I found half a tin of English toffee, which I crunched down in a glum frenzy. Then I went to the bathroom and threw up again, though so much toffee was stuck in my teeth that I probably wouldn't be able to avoid absorbing those calories. I brushed my teeth afterwards for about five minutes, flossing both before and after, hoping I had dislodged whatever chunks of candy remained.

In the mirror my face looked pale, my eyes slightly red; I put in eyedrops and slapped my cheeks lightly to bring back a little color.

A knock came at the door, and I flushed the toilet again, washed my hands, and hastened into the living room to retrieve my coat and bag. My mother's present was small enough to fit into my purse.

Anna was sleekly sealed in a bright-orange parka that managed to be at once playful and minimalist in its lines. I wished her a merry Christmas, and she gave me a sharp look. I was sure she couldn't tell that I'd just vomited, but I thought again what a pity it was that Lucy wasn't here, as she had early cottoned on to my ways and told me quite bluntly that she didn't want to keep on living with me if I was going to make myself throw up, and that I had to forswear the practice for as long as she remained my roommate; the promise she extracted from me was much easier for me to keep than a promise made only to myself, but in her absence I had slipped, fallen again into old ways. Anna would usually have kissed me on both cheeks in the European style, but I walked briskly towards the stairwell and charged downstairs so that she couldn't get close enough to me to detect, perhaps, a telltale trace of vomit.

(I was going to stop this again as soon as the holiday season was over. I hated, hated, hated the awful obsessive stream of worrying about when I would be able to purge and whether others would guess what I was doing. It was a complete waste of time and energy and terrible for the health to boot.)

We got a taxi almost at once and rode in silence over to the east side. I paid the driver (Anna offered money, but she was here at my invitation and I considered it incumbent upon me to absorb all the expenses of the occasion), let us in downstairs, and led Anna to my mother's apartment. I couldn't help but think that even my mother might be mildly taken aback by Anna's self-contained air of dangerous glamour. Anna rarely had less than three thousand dollars' worth of clothing on her back, shoes and jewelry excluded; Lucy was oblivious to this sort of thing, but it had always been one of the minor mysteries of Anna's existence. (That said, I now understood why Anna so often wore cowl-neck sweaters and shirts with mandarin collars. She had a good deal to cover up!)

"Ruth!" my mother called out when she heard me taking off my coat and boots in the hallway. "I thought you were never going to get here. What took you so long?"

"It's not like you needed my help to get the meal ready," I said snidely, hating how teenagerish I sounded. The meal itself would be catered. My mother no longer cooked, other than a few special dishes now and again, and for Christmas she preferred to order everything in, despite the fact that there would be less than a dozen of us and we could perfectly well have produced the meal ourselves at a fraction of the expense. My mother would have liked to have a huge extravagant room full of people, but our family was small: my mother and her sister weren't close, and she was pretty much estranged from the remnants of my father's family, who had not been pleased by his initial decision to marry a non-Jew and who had found nothing in my mother to overturn their original negative judgment.

My mother's close friend Nancy was there already, and the two people from the catering company were at work in the kitchen. Anna went through all the right motions, including giving my mother a silver gilt contraption with candles that she said was a Swedish Advent candlestick.

As my mother thanked her effusively, Anna brushed off her words with a graceful headshake.

"Properly, of course, I would have given this to you a month ago," she said. "In Sweden, we light one additional candle on each of the four Sundays before Christmas. Perhaps you will do so next year!"

My mother found a place for it on the mantelpiece in the living room, which was garlanded with boughs of evergreen and white flowers.

"I hadn't thought of you as particularly religious," I said to Anna.

"I am thoroughly and happily heathen," Anna said (her vocabulary was outrageous — how could she speak English like this when it wasn't even her native language?), "but the celebration of Advent in Sweden falls more under the category of cultural custom than religious observance. I prefer Midvinterblot myself. . . ."

Before I could get a chance to ask what Midvinterblot was, Nancy got up to greet me and asked to be introduced to Anna; then the doorbell rang again and we were engulfed in a sea of greetings general and particular.

While the female caterer finished the last stages of preparing the food, the male caterer-cum-bartender came around with trays of drinks; I had a glass of white wine, then another one, helping myself to a few cashews from the little silver bowl on the coffee table and savoring the combination of sharp, fragrant wine and creamy, salty nuttiness. For some reason, having Anna there as a guest was causing me to see my mother's home with new eyes. Lucy came with me there now and again too, but Lucy was domestic, familiar, an ordinary presence. Anna was an altogether different animal.

The living room — or "sitting room," as my mother preferred to call it — and dining room were joined in one vaguely L-shaped salon, with everything beautifully chosen and displayed (almost to a fault, so that one was tempted to set a china spaniel slightly awry from its companion or leave a sweater hanging sloppily over the back of a late Chippendale chair). Central to the dining room was a Welsh dresser with rows of valuable china, collected in the first instance by my mother's mother but supplemented by my mother's own forays into the antiques market; the table, highly polished at all times but now bedecked with tablecloth and centerpieces and fully set, could seat as many as fourteen with both leaves added to extend it.

The sitting room felt a little more American in its style, though the decorative scheme throughout the apartment was distinctly Anglo-American rather than continental (my maternal grandmother had been Welsh). This was in part because my mother's entire collection of nineteenth-century American toys was on display here, the most precious (mostly dolls) behind glass in cabinets but many of them not: the carved wooden Noah's Ark and barnyard sets, the tops and carts, and so forth. The dollhouses had taken over another room; they had always looked odd when juxtaposed to the other things, as they were built on more of a miniaturized scale. One shelf changed seasonally; it now had an entire crèche set up, with real straw and the three Magi approaching the Madonna and cradle with an unmistakable air of sanctity and supplication.

My mother saw Anna looking towards the toys and seized the opportunity to show them off to her. I couldn't quite stand to hear her describe each thing again, in terms more lavishly and lovingly generous than she had ever used towards anything I had ever done or made, so I let them go off together, hoping that my mother wouldn't say anything too utterly awful. It was not unreasonable to hope that with Anna she would be on her best behavior.

Nancy was kindly but irritatingly interested in hearing about my work and romantic life; I didn't mention Mark specifically, just that I'd broken something off recently and was intending merely to date rather than to settle down with anybody until I actually knew where I'd end up living. I was in the second year of a three-year postdoctoral fellowship, and there hadn't been anything jobwise worth applying for this year, though the following fall I wouldn't have the luxury of making that distinction — I would need to apply for whatever there was.

(This was a cover story, of course; it was true as far as it went, as all good cover stories must be, but I thoroughly disapprove of people who come to believe their own cover stories.)

The other guests were my mother's lawyer and his wife and their teenage son, her friend Susan, and a couple other guests who seemed to turn up year after year without actually being either intimates or family members, an antiquarian book dealer called Gerald and his boyfriend Anthony. For each of these, my mother would have chosen a perfectly tasteful and highly suitable present: a man's cashmere crew-necked sweater in a tasteful fawn, a pink leather Kate Spade iPad sleeve, a Tiffany money clip. We exchanged presents in a small way, but though my mother seemed to like the little pink pig quite a bit (at any rate she found a place for it immediately on the appropriate shelf), she liked what Gerald and Anthony brought her much better. And once she'd opened that present, I had to restrain my envy, because it was an original copy of Milton Bradley's pioneering 1860 board game *The Game of Life*. It was a checkerboard of blue and red squares, alternating between a decorative pattern vaguely reminiscent of Moorish tiling and meaningful squares on which an ominous hand pointed you from, say, Crime down to Prison or up from Industry to Wealth.

"This really is the prompt I needed," my mother said after everyone had seen it, "to purchase that display case I've been looking at. I have a few children's books I'd like to show also, and it will be safer to put these fragile, precious things under glass."

It was another step towards the inevitable translation of the apartment into a museum. Everything was meticulously selected and curated, but the sheer unrelenting accumulation of things always threatened to make the space inimical to human activity.

"Let's play the game," Anna said slyly.

Gerald looked vaguely shocked, as mint-condition antiques (toys or no) were meant to be viewed without touching, but my mother seemed willing to entertain the notion. It must have been the holiday spirit.

The game used a teetotum (a sort of spindle that ran through a multisided disk and could be twirled, very much like a dreidl) rather than a die, dice having been deemed by many nineteenth-century American game makers too strongly associated with gambling to put into the hands of the young. Anna, my mother, Anthony, and I set ourselves up around the board at one of the small occasional tables, the others gathering around us to watch.

There's no element of skill to this sort of board game. You advance along the board according to the number the roll brings you. Yet some uncanny fatality seemed to be giving my mother very bad luck and Anna very good.

"Ambition leads me to Fame," Anna remarked. She leaned over and sniffed the board appreciatively. "I like the fragrance of ancient things," she said. "A hint of mildew, but nothing for you to worry about. The condition of preservation is good."

My mother looked irked, but said nothing. She spun the teetotum, which promptly took her from Intemperance all the way back to Poverty.

In the meantime I had advanced from School to College, but had a later setback when Idleness sent me back down the board to Disgrace. It was amazing how ashamed the game could make me feel. What had I — or my avatar — done?

"This is a very puritanical game," Anna said. "It is a good thing we no longer believe that intemperance leads to ruin."

"I know it's supposed to have been outdated," I admitted, "but I guess I do partly endorse something like the notion that people are destroyed by their faults."

"Job wasn't destroyed by his faults. He didn't do anything wrong."

"That was a test. I'm not saying that in real life accidents don't happen. Of course bad things happen to good people, I'd have to be an idiot if I said they didn't. But nine times out of ten, when someone comes to a bad end, it's pretty much the consequence of their own actions."

"And I suppose you also believe that someone who succeeds in life has achieved that success on his or her own merits?"

"Of course. I could have been a lazier and a happier person, but I chose not to be. Work hard, and you'll get what you deserve."

My mother and Anna had both advanced to the top of the board again, only now my mother alighted on Idleness, which of course sent her to Disgrace on the bottom row. She audibly gnashed her teeth as Anna landed on the final square of Happy Old Age, with its fifty-point bonus.

"Well," said my mother, her lips pursed, "that was interesting."

"I will prefer to seize what I want," Anna said, "rather than act like a good girl and wait around forever for some reward that's never actually going to fall into my lap."

"Hardly an admirable philosophy," said my mother. I was mildly alarmed to find I agreed with her.

Dinner was excellent. The catering last year had been subpar, and so my mother had gritted her teeth and hired the considerably more expensive (though still affordable — she would never waste her money on one of the big fancy enterprises that charged through the nose) caterers recommended by Susan, with whom my mother coexisted uneasily in a long-standing and suffocatingly intimate rivalry. We had roast beef rather than turkey, with endearing little individual Yorkshire puddings, pan-roasted root vegetables, and Brussels sprouts sautéed with bacon and candied pecans; dessert included a particularly attractive *bûche de noël* as well as miniature mince pies and Christmas pudding with hard sauce. I had restrained myself with regard to the main course, but all this meant was that there was room for me to absolutely gorge myself on dessert. My mother exuded chilliness at the other end of the table, and buttercream has always been my downfall.

I had to loosen my belt afterwards, my stomach hurt so much, and I felt absolutely disgusting. What on earth could I do to burn it off?

The rest of the evening seemed endless. I could almost *feel* the stream of calories being absorbed through my intestines, and the thought made me so anxious that I drank two more glasses of wine, which of course only compounded the problem. Susan and Nancy would stay latest, so that they and my mother could chew over everyone's appearance and behavior together, with Nancy providing some small mitigation on behalf of each victim that would only give my mother and Susan license to descend ever deeper into cattiness. I traditionally left once everything had been cleaned up and the caterers had gone; indeed, once we'd let them out (I averted my eyes from the tip my mother gave them, which I knew would be inadequate to season and circumstances), I was able to turn to my mother and kiss her and thank her for "As always, a very lovely holiday," and begin to pave the way for our departure.

"Don't go yet, Ruth!" Susan called from the sitting room. Her face was flushed with alcohol. "I'm having such an interesting conversation with your friend Anna — she's given me some really helpful suggestions about what I should make sure to see when I take that Baltic cruise next month."

Anna looked self-possessed, beautiful. I was not sorry I had brought her, her status would perhaps slightly augment my own, but I wished that Susan and my mother were not both such harpies; beneath their tasteful blond Upper East Side well-dressed matronly personas, both of them suddenly seemed to me absolutely monstrous.

"Anna, would you like to use the powder room before you go?" my mother asked her, her manner like cut glass.

"Yes, thank you, Fiona," Anna said. I could have sworn she was enjoying this; certainly my mother seemed as frostily tormented by her own severity as Anna was impervious to it.

Ten minutes later we came out into the damp cold evening air and I heaved a huge sigh of distress and relief.

"Do you want to walk for a little while?" Anna asked. "I feel that I have eaten too much, and I wouldn't be sorry to walk some of it off."

"Yes, let's do that," I said decisively. It wasn't actually raining or snowing; we would be perfectly warm so long as we kept up a fairly brisk walking pace, and together we wouldn't actually be at risk, though on the rare occasions I found myself there on foot at night, the deserted stretch along 110th Street in central Harlem always made me feel vaguely uneasy and as though I were asking for trouble. It was a mantra of my upbringing that it was dangerous for a girl to walk about alone on anything other than the absolutely safest stretches of Park or Madison, and though I took considerable pleasure in rejecting the conventional wisdom I'd been brought up with, I felt there was a certain amount of merit to this particular position. I had grown up with the cautionary tale of the so-called Central Park jogger, a woman who had been raped and beaten almost to death in the north end of the park in the late 1980s; I had always found it odd that she had been running in such an isolated part of the park before dawn, and in the days when the park felt significantly less safe than it did now. When she later revealed in a memoir that it was partly due to an eating disorder involving compulsive exercise that she found herself in the wrong place at the wrong time, I resolved not to let my own compulsions take me into such clear and evident danger.

Anna seemed oblivious to any risk in wandering the nearly deserted streets after dark. I suppose it is true that one is less likely to get mugged on Christmas than almost any other night of the year. We had walked up Madison to 96th Street and then over to Fifth Avenue. It was slightly eerie walking along the path on the outer edge of the park; not many weeks before, I had been standing here cheering on a friend who was running the New York City Marathon for the first time, and the contrast between the bright fizzy crowds of that day and the current dark, deserted emptiness could not have been more striking.

"Shall we walk through the park?" Anna suggested.

I hemmed and hawed a little. I could not really think it was a good idea, but Anna pressed, and in the end I felt I would seem absurd if I continued to refuse. So we walked in at the next entrance and followed the path to the main loop. Strange to say there were a handful of joggers out, and even a cyclist or two. We rounded the curve downhill to the north exit on 110th Street and I suddenly remembered what I had meant to ask Anna earlier, before the exchange of presents, the excessive dinner, and my mother's trivial but bitter defeat in the game. It was strange being alone with Anna now. I wasn't sure whether I was more afraid for her or afraid of her.

"What is — Midvinterblot, was that what you called it?"

"Midvinterblot? Oh, yes, we were talking about religion. I hope your mother didn't think I was being disrespectful or flippant."

"No, I'm sure she didn't. What was it you meant, though, when you said you celebrated Midvinterblot?"

"The term itself," said Anna, taking my arm and turning towards me, her face pale under the dim light of the streetlamp we were just passing, "refers to the midwinter sacrifice. You must be familiar with the general idea — it is the sort of thing Frazer was obsessed with when he wrote *The Golden Bough* — the sacrifice of a high-value male individual, sometimes an animal but often a warrior or a priest or even a king. At Uppsala in Sweden, the center of the cult worship a thousand years ago, it seems that every eight years, one human male and seven male animals were sacrificed on the night of the full moon at midwinter; they were hanged in a sacred tree every day for nine days, reproducing the suffering of the god Odin, who sacrificed himself to learn the wisdom of the universe, suspended from the world tree Yggdrasil for nine days and nine nights with his spear in his side."

She spoke with a scholar's neutrality, but her measured, unemotional tone made me shiver. Had I really seen her spill her own blood onto the ground in front of dozens of people? The idea of the world tree Yggdrasil brought home to me that we were walking through one of the great remaining tracts of woodland in the northeastern part of the United States, almost eight hundred and fifty acres designed and planted after Olmsted's great scheme, the park now home to over twenty-five thousand trees.

"You wouldn't ever try anything like that, would you, Anna?" I said, suddenly anxious.

Anna started laughing.

"You never know what I will decide to do!" she said.

"No, really, Anna, promise me you won't hang yourself from a tree!"

"I promise not to hang myself from a tree."

The tone of mockery behind her words, though, made me wonder whether she would really consider this a meaningful promise.

We had reached the bottom of the hill by now. I was freezing.

"Let's go out the Seventh Avenue exit and see if we can't pick up a taxi," I said.

Anna shrugged.

"If you like," she said.

We stayed on the south side of 110th Street; it meant we were on the wrong side of the road for a westbound taxi, but this way we'd see one coming and be able to flag it down. All the cabs that passed, though (and they were the only cars on the street), were either off duty or already carrying passengers.

I was morally as well as thermically shivering as we toiled up the hill to Amsterdam; despite the new condo tower on the southeast corner of the cathedral precinct, there was still something terribly ominous about the way the Cathedral of St. John the Divine loomed out of the night before us. Amsterdam Avenue was quiet, and it was with relief that I turned onto 122nd Street and stuck my hand into my bag to feel for my keys.

"It's not late," Anna commented in the elevator. "Would you like to come in for a drink?"

I weighed the invitation and was surprised to find myself accepting it. My phone remained resolutely message-free, and the walk had cleared my head enough that I felt one more drink wouldn't be altogether unwelcome. The food in me was well on its way to being digested, and I had resigned myself to working off some part of the caloric overload by exercising three times as long as usual the next day.

"I have a bottle of Swedish *isvin,* do you like it?" Anna called to me from her kitchen. I was sitting on an amazing molded wood chair that I could almost swear was an original Arne Jacobsen.

"A Canadian friend of mine used to serve ice wine with dessert at her dinner parties," I said. "Actually I hadn't realized it was made in Sweden as well. I think of it as a chiefly Canadian phenomenon."

Anna retrieved two small cut-glass tumblers from the glass cabinet in the living room and we sat across from each other at the dining table. There was something almost ceremonial about the way she poured the two glasses and pushed one across the table to me.

"*Helan går,*" she said, clinking her glass against mine.

"Cheers," I said in answer, feeling the inadequacy of my Americanism.

The wine was as sweet and intense as winter itself, the winter of sugarplums and the concentrated essence of north. It brought warmth to my cheeks, and the feeling of Anna's gaze upon me also made me burn.

"You have found it difficult interacting with your mother over the years, haven't you?" she said.

"I have," I confessed. "I always seem to fall short of her exacting standards, but I am stymied as to how to change that."

She looked at me as though she were measuring me for a garment.

"Toys and games — the daughter has chosen a field of specialization that might represent a kind of homage to her mother's interests, or perhaps a challenge?"

"The kind of game I'm interested in has nothing to do with toys," I protested. "My mother's collecting is something I'm reconciled to. I hated it when I was a little girl, of course, because there were all these dolls and toy animals and so forth that I wasn't allowed to touch, let alone play with, but I'm glad she has a serious hobby to keep her busy. She's well-respected in that community, and she even publishes now and again in one of the specialist collectors' journals."

Anna was shaking her head again, this time clearly in disagreement. I didn't understand how or why she always seemed to have the upper hand.

"I am telling you what you already know: your mother's collection is painful to behold precisely because it fixes play in stasis. A toy is stripped of its essence when it is put up on a shelf and displayed as an antique. The spirit of play is a spirit of anarchy — controlled, yes, but fundamentally chaotic in its energies, despite the rules or constraints the game's players consent to observe."

"Do you know *Who's Afraid of Virginia Woolf?*" I asked impulsively.

"I have heard the name. It's a film, isn't it?"

"Yes, there's a movie version, and the original play is very often put on in colleges and regional repertory companies," I said. "It's one of the classics of twentieth-century American playwriting, I guess you'd say, like *Death of a Salesman* or *A Streetcar Named Desire.*"

"*Streetcar* I know," Anna said.

"The play features two couples; an old bitter drunken couple and a young couple. It is one of the twentieth century's great plays about games. George and Martha have a private game, but Martha breaches the rules by making the game public. In the end George comes up with an absolutely brilliant move, a move that works within the rules of their game in one way but in another sense absolutely and permanently breaches the world of the game."

"You are enthusiastic," Anna commented. "Is the film any good?"

"Yes, very good indeed," I said. "Richard Burton and Elizabeth Taylor play George and Martha. You have to watch it, I have it on DVD; I'll get it for you right now."

"Sit!" said Anna, laughing at my frenetic display of overenthusiasm. "I will not watch it tonight. There will be plenty of time for you to get it for me in the morning."

"It shows more clearly than any other work of art I can call to mind the power of games to destroy as well as to create," I said.

"But Ruth, in your own games you sometimes court that same sterile quality your mother's toys exude," Anna said softly. "Don't you want to work on the larger scale of creation and destruction, in a world where something's actually at stake, rather than always with this meticulous preservation of the proprieties?"

Normally I would have gotten angry with her, but for some reason I was able to hear the words just then without them triggering anything emotional.

"The games I'm interested in — the ones I study, and more importantly the ones I make — they aren't at all like my mother's collections," I told her. "*Trapped in the Asylum* is an imaginative and effective way of exploring real places and real history. It has a kind of vividness and life to it that's quite different from anything of hers. My games are *all about* movement and interactivity!"

"Do you really think so?" Anna asked.

"You've never played one of my games," I objected. "You have very little idea what sort of energies drive my work."

"No, I haven't played one of your games," she answered (I felt suddenly furious about the asymmetry in our relationship — why should I have played Anna's game if she wouldn't play mine?), "but I have heard you talk about them repeatedly, and I hear containment, censorship, self-repression. You have great powers, Ruth. You should see what happens when you let them off the leash."

"That sounds almost like a compliment," I said, drawn to listen to her despite my better judgment.

The buzz of the intercom broke into our conversation. Anna jumped, a real, actual physical start.

"I hate the sound of that buzzer," she confided.

"Are you expecting a visitor?" I asked her. Often delivery people or other guests pushed buzzers at random in order to be admitted to the building, and though it was obviously poor security to buzz people in without knowing who they were, it was frequently preferable to the intrusive noise of repeated buzzing downstairs.

Anna went over to the wall panel and spoke into it.

"Who is it?"

"Anna!" said a male voice. "It's me — will you let me in?"

Anna held still for a moment, almost as though she were undecided whether or not to give the visitor entry. Then she pushed the button to release the downstairs door.

She turned back towards me, taking a deep breath and letting it out again, then pulling her hands through her hair.

"Is everything all right?" I asked, concerned. I knew she didn't give out her address readily, and I had even wondered whether she might not have a stalker herself, perhaps a wealthy ex-husband; it would make sense of a few of those small anomalies that had always puzzled me about her.

"Oh, yes," she said, though she didn't sound all right. "Everything's fine."

"Who is it?"

"My brother."

"Your brother — you didn't say he was coming for Christmas!"

"I had no idea he meant to."

And a minute later she was letting him into the apartment and introducing the two of us to each other. Anders was gorgeous, even more so than Anna; the resemblance was striking, and it only seemed odd to me that they had been given such similar names, as though they were one child split into two halves.

"I will leave the two of you to have some time alone with each other," I said after the initial introductions had been performed.

They exchanged glances, then Anna said, "Yes, but I will call you in the morning to see whether you might join us for a meal sometime in the next few days."

"That sounds great."

As she shut the door behind me, I felt suddenly desolate, left out. I spent the rest of the night watching clips of *Who's Afraid of Virginia Woolf?* on YouTube and dozing on the couch. I did not want to go to bed alone. My last thoughts before I put the laptop in sleep mode and drifted off myself into oblivion were of the beautiful Anders. I wondered whether he liked to play games, and what kinds he preferred. I hoped I would get the chance to find out.

# III

# THE BACCHAE ON
# MORNINGSIDE HEIGHTS

April 30, 2011

You asked for a chronology of events.

You said you needed the document as soon as possible because of the next court date.

I've written things down in the order I remember them happening. I've pasted in relevant blog entries and forum conversations as I encountered them; I'll go back through and fill the dates in later on. I hate how fake it sounds if I write things like "he said aggressively" or "she expostulated weakly," so I've done away with all that and given you the bare words as they were spoken. Also I've mostly relegated commentary to the footnotes.[1]

I don't know that I'll be able to answer them, but certainly let me know if you have any questions.

・ ・ ・

---
1. Feel free to delete as necessary.

It was the initial week of the new semester and I'd barely made it back in time to teach my first class. My mother had died the first week of January. She was in a car accident in November; she survived for six more weeks, but she never regained consciousness, and her living will made it clear she wouldn't have wanted to be kept alive on a respirator.

I guess I am a bad daughter because all I could think about was how many days it would take to schedule the funeral and whether I could get everything done before heading back to New York for the spring semester. I was teaching a new seminar on madness and literature, and before all of this business with my mother, I had been pretty excited about it.

This isn't directly relevant, obviously. But it's what was on my mind, and it's partly why I was sort of oblivious for so long to what was really going on between Ruth, Anders, and Anna.

That week in January, I let myself into the apartment and dumped my stuff on the living room floor. Ruth had left me a note on the kitchen table: "So sorry about your mom. Can't wait to see you and catch up. Much to report!" I found the exclamation point abrasive. I went down the hall to see if Anna was home, but though I knocked then and several times a day thereafter, she either wasn't there or wasn't answering.

I taught my first class on Wednesday and had the usual rush of relief that comes from getting over the hump of the first day. I was sitting at the kitchen table eating a microwaved frozen pizza and reading the *TLS* when I heard the key in the lock. It was around 8 p.m. when Ruth called out my name and I shouted back to her, stuffing the last crust of pizza into my mouth and chewing hard. I choked on it, though, when Ruth swept down on me. She wasn't alone. On her arm was one of the most beautiful men I have ever seen in my life.

Uncontrollable pizza-crust-induced coughing led to my having to consume several glasses of water. My eyes were watering copiously as I shook the hands of the ridiculously good-looking stranger, who turned out to be Anna's brother Anders, visiting from Sweden.

They had just gotten back from skiing in Vermont, I learned. Anna was out returning the rental car. They had enjoyed a fantastic week on the slopes, or so they said, and I hated them for it. I don't know how to ski, but I still would have liked to have been invited.[2]

Ruth suggested getting dinner. I grumpily told her that I'd already eaten, but she said we didn't have to go right away and that she'd come and get me after she made a few phone calls. Anders said he was going next door to drop off his things, then kissed Ruth on the mouth. I knew Ruth and Mark had broken up in December, but I was filled with a surge of rage at Ruth's practice of going straight from one boyfriend to the next. Nothing could have made me feel less welcome at what was now my only home in the world (my mother's furniture was at an auction house, her vacant condo about to be repainted so that a realtor could show it) than Ruth having a new boyfriend.

I went to my room and crawled under the covers in the dark with all my clothes still on. Undigested pizza sat under my breastbone like a lump of resentment. I must have drifted off to sleep, but I started awake when Ruth knocked on the bedroom door and leaned around it to ask whether I was ready to go. I had to fight a strong impulse to stay in bed, but in the end I pushed away the

---

2. I don't like going away for the weekend to rustic places, and I probably would have declined the invitation, even assuming circumstances had been different. But as soon as Anders came on the scene, that very first night I met him, I felt irritable and left out. I'm not proud of this, and it may have prejudiced me against him.

covers and rolled onto my side, then swung my legs onto the floor and staggered to my feet. As I brushed my teeth, Ruth occupied herself by straightening a pile of books on my desk and trying not to exude too wild an impatience.

I remember wondering what Anders was really like beneath that carapace of beauty.

I found Ruth in the living room. She was texting intently, and continued to do so as we pulled on our coats and went down the hall to Anna's.

I had a sudden flash of social phobia and asked Ruth whether we couldn't just go out by ourselves instead. It wasn't so much that I was rationally averse to socializing, more that I was suddenly overcome with near panic at the thought of having to talk to someone I didn't already know. But she was adamant. I gave in to persuasion, though her description of Anders as "one of the most interesting and exciting people I've ever met" made her sound more like a cult member than a rational human being.

Ruth knocked on Anna's door. It took them a minute to answer. Then they burst into the hallway and seemed to surround us, though there were only two of them and we were two also. Anders took Ruth's arm, while Anna came to my side and clasped my hands in her own, pressing our forearms together and asking how I was doing. It occurred to me that it might have been partly Ruth's self-absorption that hit me so hard earlier. Anna showed herself more perceptive than Ruth about the way I might want at least briefly to be treated like a delicate convalescent rather than being so robustly flooded with other people's ongoing life.

We walked the couple blocks to Pisticci and got a table. It's an attractive restaurant, with an exposed-brick interior studded with bookcases and an almost belle epoque feel in the part where we were sitting, with dark red walls and soft lighting. Anders and Anna both ordered pasta. Ruth had a salad. I started hitting the wine pretty heavily straightaway.[3]

Only now did I notice that Ruth was wearing a sweater I hadn't seen before. It was a cream roll-neck merino pullover of a size and style that led inexorably to the conclusion that it belonged to Anders. He was much taller than Anna, of course, and broader in the shoulders. He had that perfectly proportioned, almost boyish male physique that always makes me think of Greek statuary.[4]

Anders was the opposite of physically self-contained. He had his arm around Ruth's shoulder, his hand on her knee. He couldn't stop touching her hair. At one point he even reached across the table and laid his own hand on mine for emphasis. He was telling me about a raptor he'd seen the previous summer in the archipelago outside Stockholm, the blackness of its profile against the sky and the sharpness of the plummet to earth to seize its prey. His touch made me want to pull away. I guess I don't mind someone touching me now and again, at least in the right circumstances, but I felt huge resentment at the assumption that I wouldn't mind being touched by a near stranger. I thought it must be his looks that

---

3. I always drink fairly heavily, at least compared to what people expect, but my drinking had noticeably escalated in Philadelphia after my mother's accident. In the suburbs, you have to plan in advance in order to secure that evening's liquor quota. I was in that situation in January — I'm still in it, I guess — where one bottle of wine no longer gets the job done. Unfortunately, additional drinks on top of that don't so much get you drunk as leave you with a more deeply entrenched hangover the next day. I am due for a self-imposed period of abstinence, to be initiated at an unspecified later date.

4. Of course, he and Anna *were* Greek, in some sense, Swedish upbringing notwithstanding. I guess Greece and Sweden have in common that they're both known for their tragedies — or, wait, was Ibsen Norwegian?

made him so cocky. The very softness of his fingers as they brushed against my wrist felt like an assault.

In contrast to his hands-on friendliness with Ruth and even with me, it was noticeable that he and Anna were slightly standoffish with each other, inhibited. There was definitely less physical contact than I would have expected to see between siblings.

**ME:** What are you here for, anyway?

**ANDERS:** I didn't have anything in mind when I came over, other than visiting my dear sister.

**ME:** (*grumpily*) Do you plan to stay for a long time?

**ANDERS:** (*laughing*) Anna's probably sick of me by now — but Ruth's invited me to stay as long as I like.[5]

**ANNA:** Don't you have to get back for work?

**ANDERS:** I had a couple of good set design gigs in the autumn, but work dried up this winter. I'm directing an experimental *Miss Julie* in mid-June in Finland, but it doesn't go into rehearsal until the end of May.

**RUTH:** (*besottedly*) Well, obviously you might as well be here as anywhere else!

**ME:** (*suddenly remembering*) Anna! I missed your humanities center talk. . . .

**ANNA:** It was nothing special. I might post some of it on my blog. I'll send you the link if I do.

**RUTH:** Anna's just being modest. The talk was extremely interesting, though what's even more of a pity is that you missed most of *Places of Power.*

---

5. I was now positive they must be already sleeping together. I also felt glumly and irrationally certain that nobody would want to sleep with me ever again.

**ME:** (*envious, resentful*) Was it amazing?

**RUTH:** It was amazing!

**ME:** (*bitterly*) To games, then.

**ANDERS:** My favorite toast. I'm entirely dedicated to the spirit of play.

**ANNA:** You're perfectly capable of working when you want to, you idiot. Don't make out like you're the supreme hedonist of the family, and me just a mindless drudge.

**ANDERS:** Did I call you a drudge?

**ME:** (*casting about for a way to avert conflict*) So what's happening with *Trapped in the Asylum*?

**ANDERS:** Who or what is trapped in the asylum?

**ANNA:** It's Ruth's magnum opus.[6]

**RUTH:** It's the most ambitious game I've made to date, and I think it's the best.

**ANDERS:** Can we play it?

**RUTH:** (*repressively*) It's currently in beta testing. You can take it for a spin if you really want to.

**ANDERS:** What we really should do is develop a game together, the three of us.

**ME:** Ahem.

**ANDERS:** Four, I meant to say. The four of us.

**RUTH:** What kind of game?

**ANDERS:** Something a little like Martin Ericsson's *Hamlet* piece? Anna and I played that one in Stockholm years ago. It was intense. You'd have loved it, Ruth.

**RUTH:** A game that draws material from a play, but that isn't itself theater? Interesting. Were you thinking of a particular play?

---

6. Your guess is as good as mine whether the phrasing was supposed to sound sarcastic.

**ANDERS:** Hard to go wrong with Sophocles. What about *Oedipus Rex*?

**ANNA:** That play gives me the shivers. In any case, I'd say it's too focused on the discovery of knowledge to be a good fit for the notional game.

**RUTH:** One of Shakespeare's history plays?

**ANDERS:** Old hat. Your standard role-playing game already relies on a grotesquely denatured sub-Shakespearean idiom.[7] Besides, we can't do Shakespeare again or Martin will think we're ripping him off.

**ME:** (*drunkenly, or I wouldn't have suggested anything at all*) I'm teaching *The Bacchae* in a couple weeks, for my madness in literature seminar. I've always thought it would be the perfect play to stage in Central Park.

**ANDERS:** You're a genius, Lucy.[8] *The Bacchae*! The alluring call of Dionysus, the steamroller-style destruction of Pentheus by his own suppressed desires — that's just right.

**ANNA:** Let's not do it in Central Park, though. It should be here. Morningside . . .

**RUTH:** *The Bacchae on Morningside Heights.*

**ANDERS:** Not a play, a game. A game that will feel real.

Anna's blog was always quite impersonal, more academic and theoretical than I would have expected on the basis of her personality, but when I look back now through the winter's entries, I can almost always link each post in my mind to the conversations that must have preceded and prompted it. I'm going to paste in the

---

7. Anders actually talked like this.

8. I am not a genius.

actual entries at the relevant points; they speak to Anna's frame of mind, but they also help anchor my chronology.

## ANNA'S APHORISMS

### The magic circle

January 20, 2011; 7:39 a.m.

Game designer Martin Ericsson (he prefers the neologism "larp-wright") puts players into something he calls the *ecstatic furnace,* in which "consensus reality vanish[es] completely from the mind of the participants": he achieves this effect by mobilizing what he calls "the whole liminal-ritual-cultic bag of tricks including isolation, archetypal characters, elaborate costuming, life-and-death narratives, secrecy, intoxication, and militaristic discipline juxtaposed with wild abandon." Ericsson's earlier game *Carolus Rex* had used the confined physical space of a real decommissioned submarine to represent a steampunk spaceship; *Hamlet* was played (in two separate iterations) in an old fire engine garage beneath a city park in Stockholm, with the garage standing in for an underground bomb shelter to which the court of Elsinore and a random assortment of other citizens were evacuated at the start of the game.

How did *Hamlet* work? The final three acts of Shakespeare's play served as the initial imaginative prompt, and provided background characters within the game. The play's action was transposed to an imaginary parallel version of the 1930s in which the French Revolution had been unsuccessful and Europe remained a world of industrialized feudal societies, with a socialist revolution targeted at an oligarchy that still controlled most of the main industries. The conflict that escalates over the course of the game is thus between the socialist revolutionary Fortinbras and the dying Danish Empire. Every player was assigned a character that had been written in advance by the makers of the larp, and development of these characters was collaborative between player and writer, with chunks of plot also written for the game. Rules of conduct were fixed by Swedish law, with debauched nobles drinking real alcohol but only simulating the consumption of illegal substances (i.e., powdered sugar was substituted for cocaine, but nonsimulated consensual sexual acts were allowed to take place).

The players of *Hamlet* took a vow of silence, swearing not to discuss the game in detail with anyone who was not also a participant in the game, but one player later published an evocative account of her experience. Johanna Koljonen explains that the *outcome* of the game was never in doubt. *Hamlet* was teleological, end-oriented: Fortinbras and his rebels *would* arrive, with force on their side. Dramatic tension derived instead from Hamlet's famous question *To be or not to be?* Life or suicide? Every player had to answer this question at the game's end. Some characters would over the course of the game be killed in any case, but those who remained alive at its conclusion were asked to make a decision: Fortinbras would spray bullets into the crowd, and each player's character would die unless she believed she really deserved to live. Here is what Koljonen says:

> And so depressing was this portrait of humanity that very few remained. The game was played twice; only a scattered handful of characters survived. Maybe eight, maybe five out of seventy or eighty. We did not feel at the beginning that our characters were all that evil and they did not, of course, even believe their lives were threatened until they sometime in the second act could hear the riots in the streets above them. But over these few days, a couple of weeks in game-time, we players became convinced that our characters were selfish, brutal, inhumane. That the war waged by the government, sequestered with us, was utterly unjust.

Some characters were derived from the original play text; these were alternately known as *text characters, non-player characters* or *instructed players,* and included Hamlet, Ophelia, Claudius, Rosencrantz and Guildenstern and so forth, in other words, the main named characters of Shakespeare's play. These characters were (to use Koljonen's words) "'fated,' expected to do certain things, kill or leave or fight or die, at certain points in the story," but were not necessarily principals in any meaningful sense. Particularly interesting is a new narrative method invented for this game specifically. It is called "freeze-action soliloquy": at an agreed-upon signal (in this case, the tolling of a bell), action stops and players gather to hear a text character deliver a soliloquy, perform a bit of dialogue or just convey an emotion by way of weeping. Though the larpwrights did not choose to invoke the same sort of explicit model of haunting that made *Momentum* sustainable for its players over an extended period of time, the game retained a central focus on something like the ceremony for burying the dead: the bell is traditionally associated not just with a calling together of the community for some sort of worship or in response to a state of emergency, but with aiding transitions between one state and another, most commonly from life to death but sometimes in the other direction.

*Posted in* Fiery furnaces, Hamlet, Larp, Mortality

I hated listening to Ruth and Anders having sex in the other bedroom. My state of mind almost entirely sundered me from the rest of humanity. While she was still alive, I'd often been annoyed by my mother — her strongly accented English, the frugality that prevented her from throwing away a tea bag without having used it at least three times, her unshakable conviction that my poetry should win the Nobel Prize. Now I just missed her. I made a point of avoiding planning conversations for *The Bacchae on Morning-side Heights* (henceforth abbreviated BoMH). I slept a lot, avoided my MFA friends and lived on a nutritionally unsound rotation of frozen pizza, Stouffer's lasagna, and tuna sandwiches from Hamilton Deli.

The only time I felt normal was in the classroom. We read *The Bacchae* the third week of the semester — you'll remember I said that it was my suggestion that tipped Anders into choosing that play in the first instance, so it wasn't so much coincidence as over-determination.

In class I emphasized the theme of madness, since that's the through line for the whole seminar, but there's all sorts of other stuff going on there too. The play starts like a western. An unknown stranger arrives in town. In fact it's the god Dionysus, only he's disguised as a mortal. His mother was Semele, daughter of the same Cadmus who sowed dragon's teeth. Cadmus is still king in this place. The backstory: Semele was having an affair with Zeus, and jealous wife Hera tricked her into asking Zeus to show her his thunderbolt, making it a test of his love for her; as a mortal, Semele could not survive its fire, but Zeus concealed their child Dionysus from Hera and her wrath by hiding him in an artificial womb in his own thigh.

In Cadmus' house in Thebes, though, the women are saying that Dionysus is no son of Zeus, that Semele was seduced by a mortal rather than a god, and that the whole story is just a cover-up. The strongest voice in denial of Dionysus' godhead comes from Cadmus' heir and grandson Pentheus. Pentheus hates the stranger, but he's also fixated on every detail of his face and body. He can't stop talking about how the female followers of Dionysus go off into the forest to have sex.

I opened class by asking my students how they would describe the relationship between Pentheus and Dionysus.[9]

They said:

ADVERSARIES

COUSINS

DOUBLES

OPPOSITES

Preppy blond Alexander: "It's creepy the way Pentheus is so obsessed with Dionysus."

Dark-haired beautiful Janie: "Pentheus is totally fixated on maenads having sex."

I asked what Pentheus thought about sex.

They said:

DISGUST

FASCINATION

Also:

PENTHEUS IS OBSESSED WITH SEX EVEN
   THOUGH HE ISN'T GETTING ANY

At one point Pentheus sends his men out to capture Dionysus. They bind the god — he surrenders willingly — and bring him back to the palace to be stoned to death. It is an erotic scene.

---

9. Bear with me. It's relevant, really. I don't think you can understand what happened without knowing how the play might have affected Anna and Ruth in particular. All of us, though, were steeped in it and under its influence.

Reasons Dionysus surrenders:

BESIDE THE POINT TO FIGHT

WANTED TO TEACH PENTHEUS A LESSON

Things that motivate Pentheus:

ATTRACTION TO THE FORBIDDEN

DESIRE TO SHOW THAT REASON BEATS
RELIGION, FRENZY, MADNESS

HOMOEROTIC ATTRACTION

The most amazing moment in the whole play comes when the imprisoned Dionysus tells Pentheus that the god is near at this very moment and will set him free whenever he wants. Pentheus is stubborn, obtuse. He says he can't see anything.

Dionysus says in response that the god is where *he* is, and this so infuriates Pentheus that he tells the guards to seize him.

What Dionysus says in response: "You do not know what your life is, or what you do, or who you are." It's the lack of self-knowledge that destroys Pentheus. The rest of the play is a piece-by-piece demolition of Pentheus and everything he cherishes: first Dionysus makes Pentheus go mad, and then he causes the maenads to chase Pentheus through the woods and tear him to pieces. Pentheus' mother, deluded into thinking it is the head of a mountain lion, brings her own son's head back to the palace as a trophy, and only then comes to herself and has her eyes opened to what she has done.

Other things my students said that stuck with me:

Smart redhead Lexy: "The story phrases everything in terms of family history, but it's not really a story about individual people, is it? It's more about a clash of values. Dionysus stands for madness and the irrational. Pentheus stands for reason. They pretty much have to end up in conflict."

Pink-haired Chinese American powerhouse Alicia (I sometimes thought of her as a Mini-Me): "But Pentheus is the opposite of rational. He gets angry at the drop of a hat, and he has a creepy sexual obsession with Dionysus. Dionysus definitely has better anger management skills than Pentheus does!"

Lexy: "The world needs a balance between madness and sanity, or else sanity becomes extreme and obsessive."

Janie: "The rule of Pentheus is kind of like totalitarianism: Pentheus as Hitler or Mussolini."

Alicia (in vehement disagreement): "It's Dionysus who's like Hitler, not Pentheus! Cadmus tells Dionysus at the end, after Pentheus is dead, 'you come upon us with a hand too heavy,' and Dionysus totally agrees! He just says, 'Yes, for I, a god born, was treated by you with contempt.' It's a pretty pitiful reason, isn't it? Cadmus definitely thinks so, because he says back that gods should have better self-control than mortals. That's a reproach, not a compliment. And Dionysus answers him with something that isn't even a real answer: 'Long ago my father Zeus gave his consent to this.' I would be *so* angry if someone gave that as his explanation for why he, like, made my grandson go totally insane and then killed him by making my daughter lose her mind and tear him to pieces with her bare hands."

After class I picked up a coffee in the lobby of Dodge Hall and took it to a bench outside Uris where I was unlikely to see anyone I knew. I drank it slowly, then dragged myself inside the building to the business school library and made a pitiful attempt to draft the review I was supposed to submit the following day. I was writing about a morbidly appealing book-length sequence of poems on

Egyptian embalming techniques and *The Book of the Dead,* but I totally couldn't concentrate on it. Instead I went online and found a new post up at Anna's blog.

## ANNA'S APHORISMS

### Strange fruit

January 29, 2011; 11:50 a.m.

Appendix I, "Maenadism," E. R. Dodds, *The Greeks and the Irrational* (1951):

> There must have been a time when the maenads or thyiads or βάκχαι really became for a few hours or days what the name implies — wild women whose human personality has been temporarily replaced by another. Whether this might still be so in Euripides' day we have no sure means of knowing; a Delphic tradition recorded by Plutarch suggests that the rite sometimes produced a true disturbance of personality as late as the fourth century, but the evidence is very slender, nor is the nature of the change at all clear.

*Posted in* Bacchae, Euripides, Personality, Ritual, Wild things

The phrase "true disturbance of personality" slightly frightened me. I blew another hour or so on the Internet. I didn't understand why teaching was the only thing I could pay attention to. Even coffee seemed to have lost the power of dispelling the fog that clouded my brain all the rest of the time.

Finally I gave up and went home. I am pretty sure that was the same day I passed a cluster of girls standing and texting in front of Buell Hall. I caught a snatch of their conversation as one said to another, "Buell Hall is the only remaining trace of the Blooming-dale Asylum. Do you want to pick up some more points, or should we go straight to the ward?"

They were playing Ruth's game *Trapped in the Asylum*!

The reason I remember this is that I felt angry that Ruth seemed to have lost interest in *Trapped*. I blamed Anders. His imaginative world used up all the air in the room, leaving no fuel for Ruth's own projects. Even I had been slightly hoodwinked by him. I was sure that his enthusiasm for the Euripides play and his habit of consulting me on matters literary were pure flattery and manipulation.

Back at the apartment, I found Ruth making marmalade to an aural backdrop of Beth Orton. The air was mouth-wateringly redolent of oranges and burnt sugar, the kitchen counters covered with newly sterilized jars. I was torn between pleasure at impending deliciousness and concern that Ruth was in the grip of the sort of massive culinary project, usually involving large amounts of sugar, that only struck her when she was most disordered in her eating and accordingly also in her mental health.

I gave her a closer look. She'd stripped off the bulky sweater belonging to Anders that she seemed to have been living in recently, and her tank top showed her prominent collarbones and the tiny diameter of her upper arms.

A mutual friend of ours from college died in her mid-twenties from complications resulting from a decade and a half of restricting and purging. It was not acceptable to me to think of something like that happening to Ruth.

**ME:** Ruth, I know it makes you crazy when I bug you about this, but are you sure you're eating right?

**RUTH:** I wasn't doing so well over the holidays, but I'm better now.

**ME:** That chicken in the fridge is past its sell-by date.

**RUTH:** I bought a ton of groceries just before Christmas, but I couldn't face actually cooking them. Don't say it, I'm not dumb, I know it's a waste of money to buy broccoli and organic spinach and wild salmon if I'm just going to let them rot in the refrigerator. When Anders first got here, we were eating out every night, but I think he ran out of money.

**ME:** (*wrapping two pounds of chicken breast, a bewhiskered catfish, and three or four liquefying vegetables in a double bag from Applebee's*) No need to apologize. I'll take the trash out right now. Anything else you want to chuck?

**RUTH:** No, that's fine. I'll wait until tomorrow to scrub the fridge. Anders and Anna are coming over pretty soon for drinks.

This was license to pour myself a glass of white wine. Ruth got the bottle of Absolut from the freezer, tipped a good slug into a tumbler and topped it up with soda water and a wedge of lime, a drink she liked because of its being relatively low carb.

Anna arrived twenty minutes later and said Anders would be coming soon. She had brought another bottle of white wine, which I put into the refrigerator for later. It was an Alsatian white in a long, thin, green bottle. It looked delicious, but the mere fact of its existence made me slightly uneasy. When she had come over in the fall semester, Anna usually brought red wine, not white, as that was what both she and Ruth preferred. White wine seemed to signal an attempt to cater to my preferences. There had to be an ulterior motive.

I refilled my glass of cheap sauvignon blanc and poured a fresh one for Anna. In the living room, she had already taken my own usual spot at the table by the big computer. Ruth was in the armchair, which meant I had to sit on the couch. I made myself as comfortable as I could, just preventing myself in time from resting my feet on the coffee table. It was allowable to curl one's shoeless feet up on the sofa, but not to use the coffee table as a footrest, at least according to the obscure set of Ruthian codes discerned by me over a period of several months when I first moved in.

We heard the door opening. Anders must have already had his own key. He came in and helped himself to wine, then took the opposite end of the couch from me. It was strange to be in the same room with him and Anna. They were extraordinarily similar in their looks, to the point of its being actively disconcerting.

I turned my attention to Ruth and realized that all three of the others were seething with excitement. By now I felt as though I were being triple teamed by members of a religious cult.

Anna and Ruth both looked to Anders. He threw himself on his side and reached out for my hand. I let him take it, but inwardly I was recoiling and also wondering why he would want to grab me.

**ANDERS:** Will you swear yourself to secrecy before I tell you anything more about the game?

**ME:** Swear myself to secrecy? Sure.[10]

**ANDERS:** Then swear. Swear not to breathe a word outside this room concerning any of the things whereof we speak tonight.

**ME:** OK, your language is making it hard for me to take this totally seriously, but I swear. I am a good secret keeper.

**ANDERS:** Now we drink to seal the oath.

---

10. What did they imagine they were going to tell me that would require such strict confidentiality? That Anna was secretly the Queen of the Unseelie Court and I was being tapped to serve as her fairy handmaiden?

**ME:** So what's this game going to be like?

**ANNA:** Like nothing you've ever experienced before.

**ME:** You know, I'm not really a big game person.

**RUTH:** This game's different. You see —

**ANDERS:** Play this game, and you'll never be the same again. In fact, the verb "play" is insufficient to convey what will happen to you when you immerse yourself.

**ME:** You mean like the slogan "The game plays you"? I don't really understand how that would work.

**ANNA:** Choose an affiliation. Team Dionysus or Team Pentheus?

**ME:** I don't get it.

**RUTH:** Joyful sex or repressive prohibition?

**ME:** For real? Who would choose Team Pentheus, in that case? Isn't joyful sex always preferable?

**ANDERS:** (*exchanging glances with Ruth*) Your sexual naïveté is charming, Lucy.

**ME:** (*grumpily*) I guess you're telling me there's something erotic about repression as well?

**ANDERS:** The game won't revolve around the characters of Dionysus and Pentheus in the same way the play does. We'll hear some of their exchanges, but the story will serve more as counterpoint or echo than as plot. I see the two figures as uncanny doubles, mirrors of each other.

**ME:** Doubles? You and Anna will play those parts, then.

**ANDERS:** There's a better way to do it. You're right to imagine that Anna will play Dionysus. But it's Ruth who will make by far the best Pentheus.

It was true. Something about Ruth's stern moralizing nature made the role a perfect fit. Also, though Ruth and Anders looked nothing like one another, Ruth and Anna had in their way as strong a resemblance as Anna and Anders, so that the three of them formed a strange Venn diagram of likeness.

From the *New Yorker,* Goings On About Town:

> Some little girls want to be princesses when they grow up, and Disney provides an outlet, down to the tiaras and face glitter. If you fantasize about becoming a maenad, though, group role-playing venues are hard to come by. This month, you're in luck: a Swedish theatrical impresario (who withheld his name, for fear of a crackdown from U.S. immigration authorities) is running a live-action role-playing game in Upper Manhattan that promises to release your inner Dionysian.

From the Wikipedia entry for "thyrsus":

> In Greek mythology, a staff of giant fennel (*Ferula communis*) covered with ivy vines and leaves, sometimes wound with taeniae and always topped with a pine cone. These staffs were carried by Dionysus and his followers. Euripides wrote that honey dripped from the thyrsus staves that the Bacchic maenads carried.

Anders was a reality ideologue — he wanted the game to feel more real than reality itself — but even he had to draw the line at dripping honey. If you couldn't have the honey sort of magically seeping out and then swelling forth from the top of the wand, it wouldn't be much of an effect, and in any case, the Morningside Park toilets are locked when the park officially closes at 10 p.m.; it is possible to pee in the bushes, though I will generally prefer not to, but there is nowhere to wash your hands.[11]

Players were recruited from all over the city. Ruth liked to use

---

11. If you're a maenad, you probably shouldn't be thinking about something so prudential and future oriented as hand-washing.

Facebook, while Anna had a presence on all sorts of Internet bulletin boards (mostly focused on urban exploration and related forms of metropolitan risk-taking). Anders pursued his own channels to find people who would be suitable members of a community that had to be bound largely by trust. In order to get an actual invitation, you had to be a close friend or the friend of a close friend.[12] Even I had been more thoroughly sucked in by this point than I had intended, while for the other three, the game had become all-consuming.

What we were doing in the weeks preceding the game's official debut: so-called buildup sessions. Every Friday night we met and had — well, if it were a sport, I guess you'd call it a scrimmage. We were preparing for three days of continuous play in the middle of April, a seventy-two-hour extravaganza of debauchery and competition, and we had to go beyond skills and drills and practice playing for real.

We met around ten at night at a space on Manhattan Avenue, on loan for free from a game-friendly Harlem entrepreneur. It was the whole second floor of a tenement fallen into decrepitude, a six-story walkup that would ultimately feature floor-through luxury condos. The ground-floor improvements had been completed and a small Ethiopian restaurant operated out of the storefront, but the space we used on the third floor was still just an empty shell.

Water and electricity were running throughout the building, but there was no plumbing except for one tap with a bucket be-

---

12. It is my suspicion that sociopaths populate the group of my friends' friends at rates very similar to the general population, but in the end it wasn't one of the outer circle who proved dangerous, was it?

neath it and an open drain in the floor.[13] Lighting was confined to bare bulbs running on extension cords from the two functional wall sockets, although later on Ruth hung Christmas tree lights to make the atmosphere less stark and more festive.

The door downstairs operated on a key code system. Each floor had a separate access code. You got the number by putting up a $250 deposit. This was partly to cover expenses (mostly wine and other intoxicants), but also to help the players trust one another.

We stored props — wands, drums, surplus fawnskins — in a large self-contained area at the back of the unit. Anna and Ruth had installed cheap mats and cushions for comfortable lounging. They had also placed an actual wine fountain in the middle of one wall on a concrete pedestal; it flowed with lavish infusions of a twelve-dollar Malbec Anna bought by the case.

I couldn't tell you exactly which night it was, but here's what happened the first time I remember things really taking off. This will give you the basic template.

The air was filled with clouds of pot and cigarette smoke. Three girls were actually writhing on the floor beneath the fountain so that they could drink directly from it. If you wanted to go crazy, you certainly got the sense that it would be encouraged rather than inhibited in this increasingly Dionysian atmosphere.

Anna was standing on an upended plastic bucket in the corner, neck arched and throat bare as she tipped her head back to drain the last of a pitcher of wine. The blood-red stains around her lips reminded me strongly of John Hurt as Caligula in *I, Claudius*.

---

13. I saw people peeing in it more than once, not just men either, and the smell of urine was noticeable in the stairwell. This makes the place sound more squalid than it seemed at the time.

She leaned down and said a word to the young man beside her, who began tapping on his drum, first lightly, and then with increasing volume and momentum.

**ANNA:** Team Dionysus![14] To me! Let us take our celebrations outdoors to Morningside Park.

**RUTH:** (*standing on a milk crate at the opposite end of the room*) Team Pentheus! Let the maenads go unmolested. We will track and capture them easily when the time comes.

**ANNA:** You should disperse once we reach the street. Keep a low profile heading into the park. If a cop stops you and asks what you're doing, be ready to show a government-issued ID. Choice of a cover story is up to you. You probably won't want to say anything like "I am a worshiper of Dionysus, come to celebrate his glory" (*laughter*), but you might say something about an ethnographic project or a fitness class.

**RANDOM TEAM MEMBER:** What's our mission for tonight?

**ANNA:** To celebrate the god Dionysus and the sacred madness he bestows. It is illegal to drink alcohol in the park. Drink up!

The rest of the night is kind of a blur, not just because of how much alcohol I drank. I was running with a bunch of other women along Manhattan Avenue and then into the park; we passed an older woman at the bus stop who stared at us as though we had come from another planet. We were all wearing fawnskins and very little else, traditional garb of maenads everywhere.

We chased each other around the park. Some of the strangers

---

14. I can't remember if I said so already, but obviously I was a member of Team Dionysus. I went and clustered with a bunch of others around Anna. It was perversely reminiscent of lining up in teams for elementary school gym class.

we encountered made sarcastic comments, but others joined our revelry. We drank some more. There were drums and dancing, and a teenage boy with a tin whistle. I saw a maenad with a python around her neck. That garland of serpents thing is an ancient component of the iconography of maenadism, and I wondered whether it would be possible to get a whole mess of garter snakes and fix them into some kind of a headdress, but I dismissed the idea when I thought how traumatic it would be for the poor little creatures.

Anna was dancing around the edge of a larger group, the fawn-skin falling off her shoulders. She tapped first one dancer and then another with her thyrsus. At some point we got tired of being outside and ran back to the lair, still in a sort of controlled frenzy.[15] The building was empty, and I remember wondering how Team Pentheus had spent the evening. There were about a dozen of us, I guess, and we took over the space pretty effectively, collapsing on the low foam divans and cushions with wine and water, which was all we needed.

I'm not sure how much to tell you about the next part, and the only reason I've put it in is that you promised me nobody would see this document but you and your assistant. It speaks more immediately than anything else I could write to the way the nights of the game changed us. You have to understand, I'm not the type of person who does this kind of thing![16] Somehow, though, there I was on a heap of cushions with a supremely attractive man. His

15. We didn't use the term *lair* ironically. We preferred it to the more infantilizing *clubhouse* as a straightforward descriptor, though clubhouse tended to be the natural default usage.

16. I didn't lose my virginity until my sophomore year of college. I'm not bad-looking, but I am a solidly built and distinctly nerdy Taiwanese American poet and suitors aren't beating down the door.

name was Claude, and he hailed from the French Antilles; he had a wiry fit body, light brown skin, and a tight head of short nappy curls. He was wearing triathlon shorts; I had on my Lululemon yoga pants and a Nike sports bra, with only a thin tank top between that and the fawnskin, which couldn't be said to provide much coverage. We were lying down next to each other and his hand was down my pants and although there were people right next to us we were pretty much actually having sex. Only when he whispered to me that we should go somewhere more private did I suddenly start upright, pull the top back down over my stomach and take his hand out of my pants.

I felt extremely self-conscious, not just about the last half hour but about the whole evening. What had happened to me? How had the hours passed so quickly? I gave him an embarrassed goodnight kiss on the cheek and went to get my things from the rack at the back of the floor-through. I had to turn my eyes away from two other couples. Anna had a girl in her lap, a beautiful girl, and was stroking her hair and singing her some kind of a lullaby; I took this as partial confirmation of Anna's conjectural lesbianism, though I still don't feel like I understand everything about Anna's sexuality, the mix of self-assertion and self-destructiveness that might have driven her choice to have sex with one person as opposed to another.

The walk home was freezing. I didn't have my phone and I wasn't wearing a watch, but it must have been 4 a.m., as the bars on Amsterdam were just closing and I had to endure some catcalls from patrons spilling drunkenly out into the street. But my keys were still safely stowed in the little inside pocket of my yoga pants, and it was a huge relief to get to the lobby and find the empty elevator waiting there to take me upstairs. I was glad I didn't have to share it with anybody, as my skin smelled of sex and cigarette smoke, a dense musky overlay that reminded me vividly and nostalgically of undergraduate life.

I thought I would take a shower, but I had to modify my plan when I found Ruth sobbing on the couch in the living room. If it were me, I'd rather weep in privacy, but it seemed inconsiderate to leave her alone, so I sat down awkwardly and touched her on the shoulder. I was taken aback when she turned to me and clasped her arms around my neck like a child holding on to its mother. Usually Ruth keeps everything safely in check; she is prone to fits of self-loathing, stringent self-discipline and/or self-castigation more intense than anything that ever strikes me, but she never cries, and her stated position on things is always that they are under control, a phrase she uses so often it could be her personal motto.

**ME:** *(hoping the smell of cigarettes would drown out the smell of sex)* What's wrong?

**RUTH:** Nothing. Only I feel so upset!

**ME:** Is it something to do with Anders?

**RUTH:** *(mildly indignant)* Of course not. Why would you say that?

**ME:** *(backtracking)* No reason in particular.

**RUTH:** What do you really think of him, anyway?

**ME:** Of Anders?

**RUTH:** Don't stall. Of course I'm talking about Anders!

**ME:** *(stalling)* I haven't spent enough time with him to have formed an opinion.[17]

**RUTH:** Lucy, you're the queen of the snap judgment.

---

17. False! What I really thought was that Anders had brainwashed her, or at least mobilized the full and not inconsiderable force of his personality to get her to act against her own interests. That said, it was eminently suitable that Ruth should be in charge of Team Pentheus, a representative of reason and control and an enemy of Dionysian abandon.

ME: That's not fair!

RUTH: He's gorgeous, isn't he?

ME: (*relieved I can agree*) Yes, gorgeous. Absolutely and amazingly good-looking. He must work out quite a bit, too. Even with good genes, people don't keep on looking like Greek gods in their thirties unless they exercise.

RUTH: He's incredibly fit. Do you think he's really in his thirties, though? I'd have said twenty-eight, tops.

ME: Well, he's Anna's older brother, isn't he?

RUTH: Oh, no.

ME: I'm sure Anna said that though they were mistaken for twins when they were kids, her brother's a year and a half older.

RUTH: Lucy, there's something we have to talk about.

ME: Anna's age?

RUTH: I'm serious. I do think Anna lied about which one of them is older, but that's not the real issue. I'm afraid that Anna herself isn't quite what she seems.

ME: I'm afraid like "I think it is vaguely possible," or "I'm afraid" like you're positive and trying to break it to me gently?[18]

RUTH: Anders says Anna has pretty major mental health issues.

ME: Anders didn't say "mental health issues." Those words have a distinctly Ruthian and American cast!

---

18. I can't say I'd never wondered myself about those minor mysteries of Anna's self-presentation. Given what had presumably been a pretty squalid upbringing, how did she come to have so much money? Why was she so reticent about her private life? But I *liked* Anna, liked her in a way that made this sort of speculation unproductive. I have been friends with Ruth ever since our junior year of college when we met in a French history class at Penn — Ruth was at Bryn Mawr, but she took a lot of consortium classes — and I know her as well as people know their siblings. What I really thought at this point was that Ruth herself must be aware, on some level, that these words were an attempt to drive a rift between me and Anna. It made me especially grumpy that she should be doing this even as she consolidated her own bond with Anders.

**RUTH:** The exact phrasing doesn't matter. She's been diagnosed with borderline personality disorder —

**ME:** Practically half the girls we knew in college had a borderline diagnosis at one time or another.

**RUTH:** (*overriding the objection*) Anders says she's a liar. Her position in Copenhagen is real, but she lied repeatedly to get there, lied and forged credentials.

**ME:** Are you saying Anna's an imposter? Don't you think the Fulbright people would have checked her credentials thoroughly? Unless she's lying about the Fulbright.

**RUTH:** The Fulbright's for real. I called the program office to check. I'm not saying she's literally an imposter. I've seen the picture on her passport, and I'm positive she and Anders really are brother and sister. But Anders says she never got an undergraduate degree. And she committed crimes as a young teenager that would have been prosecuted as felonies if she'd been an adult.

**ME:** (*sick to my stomach*) What crimes?

**RUTH:** He wouldn't say, and I assume the records would be sealed because of her being underage, at least if it's anything like the United States. It sounds pretty bad, though. He also hints that she made a bundle selling drugs in her twenties, though when I pressed him on that, he didn't seem to think she was still dealing. Most of all, he says we shouldn't trust anything she ever says about herself. Apparently she's a pathological liar.

**ME:** Why is he telling you all this?

**RUTH:** He can see I've been getting pretty close to Anna, and he doesn't want me to get hurt.

**ME:** Don't get mad, but how do you know Anders is telling the truth? It's only his word against Anna's. We've known her longer, and I like her so much. Why did he come to stay with her in the first place, if he thinks she's such a shifty character? Isn't it a little hypocritical of him to warn you against her?

RUTH: Actually, he does think he's outstayed his welcome at Anna's. You don't mind if he moves in with me, do you, Lucy?

ME: (*furious but struggling for the appearance of equanimity*) It's your apartment. You can invite whomever you like.

RUTH: Obviously he'll stay in my bedroom, not in the living room, though I expect he'll take over a small area here for his things.

ME: (*miserably*) Sure. Have you talked to Anna about any of this, by the way? Given her the chance to defend herself?

RUTH: (*sharply*) There's no need to take that tone. All I'm saying is that you should be careful. It's fine if you like her. She's a very charming person. But that doesn't mean she can be trusted.

She yawned then, and I said goodnight (by that point it was actually light outside), and went to take a shower before falling into my bed.

At that point I would have described the thing between Anna and Anders as a he said, she said that came down to ancient history. There were deep-seated questions of character and temperament, questions I didn't imagine could ever be answered with any clarity. One thing that was clear, though, was that Ruth had no impulse to doubt the word of her irresistible new beau. Much easier, for Ruth, was to counter the possibility that Anna might be a sociopath by pulling back and distancing herself from her.

When I got up the next morning, Ruth had already gone to the office. Anders was nowhere in evidence either. I checked my email, but found only a few questions from students and a slew of ads and announcements. Anna had texted me ("did u like last nite?") and I sent her back a brief affirmative.

I was drinking my coffee at the kitchen table when a knock came at the door. It was Anna, who looked invigorated rather than drained by the previous night's bacchanals.

**ANNA:** Can I come in?[19]

**ME:** Yes, of course. Have you eaten breakfast?

**ANNA:** I'd have a coffee and a slice of toast, maybe.

**ME:** Coffee I can do, but there isn't any bread. Ruth has certain carbs under prohibition right now, and bread's not allowed into the house. Yogurt and marmalade?

**ANNA:** Just coffee, then. It was fun last night, wasn't it?

**ME:** Oh, yes, definitely.

**ANNA:** This is just the beginning. You're not going to believe how intense this stuff can get. I saw the potential during the *Hamlet* game in Stockholm, and something even more transformative may take place here. I wanted to mention: We're going to have to do a better job isolating ourselves from Team Pentheus for the duration of the game. It's natural for there to be a good deal of communication in the planning stages, but we have to remember that our interests and theirs are profoundly at odds.

**ME:** I can't help talking to Ruth sometimes about the game.

---

19. Traditionally the vampire has to have explicit permission to cross the threshold, and Anna's question felt a lot like that sort of a request. I'm not sure what it was about her that always made me think superstitiously, mythologically; she was so modern in her demeanor and dress, but she evoked a power that harked back to older forces. In the light of day, Ruth's suspicions about Anna seemed gothic, far-fetched, and yet I had long found Anna both of those things herself.

**ANNA:** You have to take sides, Lucy.

**ME:** But the game won't last forever. It will all be over in a few weeks.

**ANNA:** Yes, but games have consequences. They change us.

**ME:** (*uncomfortable, striving to change the subject*) I am going to bring my own bottle of champagne next week and let it flow freely over my face and throat.

**ANNA:** That's right, you don't like red wine, do you? The visual effect of red is more dramatic, though. Champagne doesn't give the same jolt.

**ME:** It's a silly question, but do you think these fawnskins are machine washable?

**ANNA:** I made sure when I bought the material that it could go into a washing machine without being destroyed, though I recommend hanging it to dry rather than putting it in the clothes dryer.

**ME:** Certainly I cannot afford shrinkage. Mine is quite skimpy enough as is.

**ANNA:** It should be warmer by the time we're playing the game for real.

**ME:** It's not bad now, though, is it? Were you cold last night?

**ANNA:** No, but some of the girls were complaining about it on Twitter this morning. #BoMH, if you're curious to see what else they're saying.

I was tempted to ask her questions about the beautiful half-naked Claude, so that I could figure out who knew him and how I might see him again outside of the game, but there was also something hugely appealing about the sharpness of the line as it had been drawn between the world of the game and the world of real life. If I saw him again, I realized, that would be fine, and if I didn't, the memory of the experience would be preserved as one of the most unusual and certainly the most brazen sexual encounter I had ever had in my life.[20]

Anna declined my suggestion that she should come with me to early-afternoon yoga. In class, my limbs felt unusually stiff and sore from the previous night's exertions, though sun salutations soon loosened the backs of my thighs and I could feel everything warming up and becoming more limber through and over the soreness.

After class, I was slow to roll up my mat and gather my other belongings. Another woman was still retrieving her possessions from an adjacent spot on the wall, and I thought I saw a notebook cover I recognized.

**ME:** That was your book!

**STRANGER:** (*taken aback*) Excuse me?

**ME:** I found your journal after class here a while ago. I left it at the front desk. Obviously you must have found it again.

**STRANGER:** Yes! I write or draw in it constantly, so I freaked out when I realized I'd left it somewhere. I don't go that many places, though, so this was the first place I looked. Thanks for handing it in to the front desk.

**ME:** I did open it up to see whether your name and number were written at the front, but I tried not to look at anything else. I know a book like that is ferociously private.

**STRANGER:** I'm Jami, by the way.

**ME:** Lucy.

---

20. Even aside from the sexual component, the game was the sort of thing I would have concealed from my mother. The fact of no longer needing to downplay the more disreputable elements of my life gave me considerable pain. I missed having her to not tell things to.

We shook hands, an oddly formal gesture after the impersonal intimacies of yoga class, and ended up getting coffee and bread and jam at the Silver Moon Bakery downstairs. I can't explain exactly how it happened, but I ended up not just telling her about the game but actually recruiting her for Team Dionysus. After extorting a promise that she would come to the next Friday night practice, I was not sure whether to feel proud or queasy at having become part of the game's mechanism of propagation.

Jami's addition made the subsequent Friday's session of Dionysian frolicking even better fun than the last one had been. We ran around the park and clambered on boulders and drank rum from Claude's flask; he and I went much further in terms of outdoor semipublic sexual contact than I would ever have thought plausible. Jami lived near me in the upper 120s, and when things had finally begun to wind down, she and Anna and I walked home together along Amsterdam Avenue. We passed a bar that looked hospitable and decided to stop in for one more drink. Anna was in a strange mood, high on adrenaline and who knows what else, alternating between excessive friendliness and acute irritability.

It was not really a coincidence, I suppose, as there aren't a ton of bars along that stretch, but we found Ruth and Anders already drinking at a table in the corner. It was deemed appropriate for us to join them despite the interteam communication embargo.

**ANNA:** The game's threatening to get a bit boring.

**RUTH:** Boring? You don't mean that, do you, Anna? I can't tell you exactly what we've been doing, obviously, but it's pretty amazing. I bet most of Team Dionysus feels the same way about whatever you guys have been up to.

**ANNA:** I do mean it. Boring. And you know what happens when I get bored.

**RUTH:** Actually, I don't know.

**ANDERS:** (*smirking*) Bad things! Bad things happen when Anna gets bored. That's right, Anna, isn't it?

**ANNA:** (*ignoring him*) The battle between Dionysus and Pentheus should have an occult dimension. We're in the same physical space as *Places of Power.*[21] Why shouldn't some of the same conditions still be operative? Grant's Tomb probably needs resecuring by now.

**RUTH:** How would that work? Another big ritual?

**ANNA:** No. Or, rather, not exactly. Team members keep score on their own, executing individual moves to build up the psychic fortifications. We can use the same online forum as for all the other BoMH stuff, and we'll set up a password-protected group for each team where members can log extra-game activities.

**ME:** Keep score? But what are they keeping score *of?* I'm missing something.

**ANNA:** (*grinning*) Can't you guess?

**JAMI:** Tell us, Anna! I'm totally in the dark also.

**ANNA:** I would have thought it was totally obvious. If you're for Dionysus, you shore up failing wards of protection by having wild sex in Morningside Heights locations, preferably outdoors.

**JAMI:** You do *what?*

**RUTH:** You think people will actually log their sexual activity?

---

21. I can't speak to this game directly. Shorthand version: demented Morningside Heights–based urban exploration along *Ghostbusters* lines.

**ANNA:** I am sure they will. First off, it's an important part of the game. I'm also going to sell everybody on it by offering incentives. Best sex act in the first round of posting wins an iPod shuffle.

**ME:** What do you mean by "best"?

**ANNA:** Let's say each given act will be evaluated by two independent judges on the criteria of originality and risk-taking.

**RUTH:** Let me make sure I have this right. You think people will write truthful posts about real sex that they actually have? How will you know they're not lying?

**ANDERS:** A handful might lie. Most of them, though, will be liberated by having a pseudonymous forum for logging relevant exploits. Trust me, I've seen it happen before.

**JAMI:** And what about Team Pentheus? What will they have to do to get points?

**ANNA:** That's up to Ruth and Anders to decide.

Anna and I left before Ruth and Anders were ready to go, so I didn't see my roommate again until later the next morning. I had a headache when I got up, the inevitable consequence of steady drinking over a period of six or seven hours, but in every other respect I felt surprisingly cheerful. The game was good for my spirits. It had finally caused the fog of death-related depression to lift.[22]

Ruth was gone, and Anders didn't seem to be around either (he had shown himself to be surprisingly tactful about not hanging around the apartment when she wasn't home), so I surreptitiously rooted around in the fridge until I found an almost empty jar of

---

22. "Death-related" sounds a little stark, but the word "bereavement" makes me want to throw up. Also, if one more person told me how sorry they were that my mother had "passed," I was going to scream. It's not just gruesomely euphemistic. It's also totally ungrammatical.

strawberry-rhubarb jam. I ran a spoon hard along the bottom edge and slid the jam directly into my mouth, but it didn't sufficiently sate my desire for sugar, so I rummaged further until I came across a jar of lemon curd Ruth had used for sponge sandwich cakes a few months earlier. It was surely wrong to spread something so dessert-like on bread. It should be eaten on its own, the concentrated pure essence of sweet, nothing superfluous.

It was with a guilty start that I heard the key in the lock at the front door. I slammed the jar back in the fridge and dropped the spoon in the sink.

Ruth was breathless and ruby cheeked, back from her morning run. She poured herself a glass of water from the Brita jug on the counter.

**ME:** It's amazing the way you get out there first thing in the morning! We weren't home till after four last night.

**RUTH:** (*dispassionately*) You'd find it easier to get up in the morning yourself if you didn't drink so much.

**ME:** That's mean!

**RUTH:** I'm not drinking at all during the game.

**ME:** You're not drinking? What did you have in front of you last night at the bar?

**RUTH:** (*smugly*) Club soda. Drinking isn't in character.

The talk of whether or not things were in character was one of the bits I found most tedious about the serious larpers. Ruth's role as Pentheus seemed to have affected her very strongly, or at least its manifestations were more pronounced than the Dionysian overlay seemed to have been in Anna's case.[23] She'd taken to tidying up my

---

23. But then Anna was already quite Dionysian to begin with.

papers in the living room without asking, including "accidentally" throwing away some pages of scribbled notes for a new poem. She argued with Anna incessantly about every particular of the game and its logistics. Only Anders was immune to her self-righteous criticisms.

I still didn't understand the sway he had over Ruth. Was it sexual magnetism? It seemed less to do with physiological responsiveness than with an almost moral tug on Ruth's part towards Anders. Whatever it was, I didn't like it. Nor did I enjoy my sense that the underlying dynamic between myself and Ruth, already affected by Anna's arrival in September, had tipped over into something actively fraught with Anders' advent.

Ruth had finished stretching out her quads and was now loosening the hamstrings by resting each leg in turn on the counter. Her stretching routine was a thing of beauty, due to a childhood of ballet and gymnastics. She had gorgeous form and really remarkable flexibility, as well as that dancer's build that comes only from years of work plus genetic giftedness. I couldn't help staring as she raised her right leg all the way up to her shoulder and then back behind her right ear. It was more like what a cat does than something anatomically possible for a human.

RUTH: Something's on your mind.

ME: (*deflecting*) If drinking isn't in character, it's just as well I'm not a member of Team Pentheus.

RUTH: Do you want to go out for breakfast? It won't take me long to shower. I can be ready to go in twenty minutes.

ME: I had some jam already, but I guess that doesn't really count as breakfast. Let's go to Kitchenette, if it's not too crowded. If it is, we'll walk down the street to that weird Dutch place instead.

**RUTH:** Flemish.

**ME:** Will Anders want to come too?

**RUTH:** As far as I know, he's still asleep on Anna's couch.

**ME:** Oh?

**RUTH:** He didn't stay here last night. We're not spending nights together before game play. It's not right for members of Team Pentheus to have affectionate sex. Anders mentioned it first, but I quite agree.

We got a table at Kitchenette. Ruth was eating high-protein and low-fat and ordered an egg white omelet and a side of fruit, after a slightly tiresome exchange with the waitress in which she attempted to determine the fruit's glycemic index. I had eggs over medium and pancakes, which I doused in syrup. Ruth watched avidly as I ate them, and I took a certain satisfaction in knowing that in a world without consequences, she would much rather have been eating pancakes as well.

**RUTH:** I don't want to hear anything about what the game was like for you last night, by the way. It's important for me not to have a clear sense of what's going on for Team Dionysus.

**ME:** It gets pretty crazy out there.

**RUTH:** Don't tell me!

**ME:** Do you think it will be more of the same, once we're playing the game for real, or will it somehow be different?

**RUTH:** I don't know. Anders says it will be different.

**ME:** Yes, but what do you think?

**RUTH:** Stop pestering me with questions!

Ruth headed to her office, and I went home. I spent the day quietly, catching up on grading and scanning the paranoid maze of Daniel Schreber's *Memoirs of My Nervous Illness* for our next madness and literature seminar. I went for a short swim at the Columbia pool mid-evening, picked up take-out sushi en route home and ate it in front of the computer at the living room table. Partway through a pleasant session of Internet time wasting, I went to the BoMH site to check out the Dionysus thread. I was pretty much staggered by what had already accumulated in the way of posts about shoring up protective wards. Everyone had an alias, of course, and I supposed the anonymity might equally facilitate confession or confabulation.

### Alceste
I met a guy at the rooftop bar at the Heights and we walked down into Riverside Park and had sex behind that weird little building around 108th Street. A squirrel came and stole the half-eaten Clif Bar out of my backpack.

### Endymion
Blow job from a stranger in the Fairway parking lot, 4:30 a.m. Organic radishes on sale, $1/bunch.

### Electra
Got fucked in the Bible Garden in the grounds of the cathedral. An unearthly yell came out of the undergrowth beside us — I almost shit my pants — but it was just one of the cathedral peacocks. . . .

I did not feel inclined to write anything myself (my alias was Cassandra). It again occurred to me to wonder what on earth they could have chosen as a counterpart activity for Team Pentheus. "Had brutally effective enforcement of the regime of reason" did not convey at all the same sort of flavor.

Around 11:30 p.m., I shut down the computer, brushed my teeth, and went to bed. I felt unusually drowsy and contented, to the point where I suspected I might have become somewhat dependent on the game for a sense of well-being. I'm not sure if the game was making me sleep better than usual or if it was just the perennial benefit of a late night out drinking on Friday and a slightly hungover quiet Saturday ensuring deep easy sleep later that night. Alternately, it might just have been the Benadryl I took before bed for my allergies.

I was woken up around 1 a.m. by the sound of voices in the living room. I got up to pee, but I left the light off so as not to interrupt the flow of sleep chemicals in the bloodstream.

The voices belonged to Ruth and Anders. The tone of the conversation was quiet and steady, except when Ruth's voice rose once or twice to a higher pitch.

**RUTH:** What about afterwards?
**ANDERS:** I don't know. What about it?
**RUTH:** Would you stay?
**ANDERS:** It depends.
**RUTH:** Depends on what?
**ANDERS:** Depends on my sister and whether or not she'll let me.
**RUTH:** She doesn't need to have any say in the matter. You can stay with me.
**ANDERS:** I know. It's complicated, though. There is one thing you can do for me.

And at that point, at the crucial moment, I sneezed. Anders asked Ruth whether she'd heard anything and I raced back to bed, heart pounding. I fell asleep again quickly enough that when I woke up in the morning, I wasn't entirely sure I hadn't dreamed the whole exchange.

In the kitchen, Ruth was already sitting at her laptop and reading the Team Pentheus threads. When I sat down across from her, she slammed down the top of the computer and gave me a defiant look.

**ME:** I thought I heard Anders here last night.[24]

**RUTH:** I hope we didn't wake you up.

**ME:** I was just up briefly to use the bathroom. How are things looking for this coming weekend?

**RUTH:** I'm excited, but I'm also worried about attracting police attention once we're spending so much time in the park over three consecutive nights.

**ME:** It hasn't been a problem so far.

**RUTH:** I know. I have to admit I'm surprised, but it's exactly what Anders said. The police don't bother with upper middle class, mostly white people who are not actually hooligans.

**ME:** (*impulsively*) Ruth? Have you ever felt that there's something odd about the relationship between Anders and Anna?

**RUTH:** Odd in what way?

**ME:** When Anders was first here, he warned you against Anna, but what he's doing now essentially involves egging her on. She gets pretty crazy when she's playing the game, but if she's really mentally unhinged and he knows it, isn't it irresponsible of him to encourage her?

**RUTH:** It's her intensity that makes Anna such an interesting person, though, isn't it? I wouldn't call it crazy. I'd say she just

---

24. This was slightly obnoxious. I didn't want to ask outright, but I was curious as to whether Ruth still thought of herself and Anders as going out, or whether the theoretically sex-free period was more in the nature of a relationship hiatus, even perhaps a relationship quietus.

has an unusual ability to concentrate energy in the interest of higher play.

**ME:** Has Anders said anything more about Anna's lying?

**RUTH:** Bits and pieces. Nothing I feel comfortable passing on.

This conversation left me feeling distinctly uneasy. During some crucial lapse of attention on my part, the bonds between the four of us had undergone a permanent shift. Anders had detached Ruth for his own purposes and set Ruth and Anna against each other, leaving Ruth increasingly isolated from me, and perhaps from everyone else as well. Was Ruth really all right? What if the whole game was partly a stratagem on Anders' part to get Ruth under his thumb? I couldn't afford to lose another important person in my life.

## ANNA'S APHORISMS

### Daemons

April 11, 2011; 12:53 a.m.

From Friedrich Nietzsche's *The Birth of Tragedy,* a passage that has haunted me since I first read it as a teenager:

> There is an old saying to the effect that King Midas for a long time hunted the wise Silenus, the companion of Dionysus, in the forests, without catching him. When Silenus finally fell into the king's hands, the king asked what was the best thing of all for men, the very finest. The daemon remained silent, motionless and inflexible, until, compelled by the king, he finally broke out into shrill laughter and said, "Suffering creature, born for

a day, child of accident and toil, why are you forcing me to say what is the most unpleasant thing for you to hear? The very best thing for you is totally unreachable: not to have been born, not to exist, to be nothing. The second best thing for you, however, is this: to die soon."

I have shut off comments for this post so that nobody can tease me for quoting Nietzsche.

*Posted in* Daemons, Mortality


Night one: Thursday.

The room was packed. It was very obvious whether people had aligned with Dionysus or Pentheus. More than half of us, and most of the women, wore the disheveled fawnskins and leafy crowns of Dionysus. Team Pentheus seemed stronger and more ominous in its presence, though, than it had before. We had come to call its members the enforcers. Their uniform took longer to be consolidated than our own, but that night it had finally gelled and they were dressed something like Mussolini's Blackshirts, with combat boots and quasimilitary cargo pants. A few of them had antique gas masks, which I hoped were purely decorative: steampunk totalitarianism.

The enforcers left first. Ruth was at their head and Anders hovered at the back of the pack like a cyclist sweeping stragglers in a group ride. The maenads followed close behind; we were laughing maniacally and racing in smaller groups around the marching double column of uniforms. Anna periodically dashed ahead, taunting the enforcers. Once we reached the park, they would give chase, while our job was to help her evade their grasp for as long as possible. The night would end with the capture of Dionysus.

The park felt genuinely wild. I ran and called out the Dionysian EVOE and dragged an enforcer into the bushes to kiss him, Claude watching and goading me on. Then I was running again with some girls in fawnskins I'd never seen before. I spotted Anna a few times, but she effortlessly continued to elude whichever enforcers came near her.

There would be no fun to the game, though, if she were able to escape capture indefinitely. I couldn't tell how the instruction was passed along, but we found ourselves converging on a spot by the pond at the north end of the park, Anna at our head.

**RANDOM MAENAD** #1: We will call up all of your followers, Dionysus.
  You will lead a parade of us, we will be your train —
**RANDOM MAENAD** #2: We will attend you even as you are captured
  and taken to prison!
**DIONYSUS:** Let the drumming begin!


Three of the others had small drums hanging on straps from waistbands or bandoliers, and they began pounding them now, first quietly and then harder, faster.

EVOE EVOE EVOE EVOE EVOE EVOE EVOE EVOE EVOE

We began to hear activity a little farther away — the shouts of the enforcers, some thumping and muttering as they made their way towards us through the undergrowth — and we started to run together. We cried out and chanted and laughed. We slowed down only to tip more wine down our throats; I had decanted mine into a plastic sports drink bottle, so that a sympathetic officer might countenance the fiction of legality.

At the designated spot, four revelers actually picked Anna up off the ground. Two of them held her from behind while the other two cupped her feet in their hands, her knees hanging over their forearms. She was gabbling in a language I couldn't understand but that I thought must be Greek, shouting the name of the god and rousing us all to increasingly wild calls of EVOE.

Suddenly we came to a halt. I almost crashed into the maenads in front of me, and the girl behind me slammed into my back. We were a *throng,* I remember thinking. Our voices rose together as we called out in celebration of the god.

At Anna's feet were two girls carrying flashlights with red filters. They shone them up in her face, producing a sort of darkroom effect. It reminded me vividly of a scene from a movie that traumatized me as a child, the television adaptation of Lois Duncan's novel *Summer of Fear.* The protagonist's cousin turns out to be a witch, and at the climax of the movie the protagonist is working fiercely hard to develop photographs that will show the cousin *doesn't appear on film;* in the meantime, the evil cousin is actually clawing her way through the locked door of the darkroom, the scene bathed in precisely this sinister frenetic blood-colored glow.

The enforcers were coming. They chanted, the whole team of them, as they marched down the hill towards us: PENTHEUS THE RULE OF REASON PENTHEUS PENTHEUS THE RULE OF REASON

**DIONYSUS:** Stand down. They have come. Let them take us. We need not resist.

The enforcers, mostly male, were built on a larger scale than we were. Three of them swarmed over Anna, tearing her from the hands of the worshipers and pushing her face down on the ground, then pulling her hands behind her back and cuffing her wrists with plastic restraints. Ruth stood at a distance supervising, her expression cold as she shouted directions to her subordinates.

Around me, the other maenads had gone quiet. A splinter group had run off on their own, clearly with no intention of being captured and dragged back to the Manhattan Avenue lair. I didn't know whether they intended to stay out here or whether they would make their own way back to witness the confrontation between Dionysus and Pentheus. In a strange way, the logic of the game called for there always to be worshipers of Dionysus out in the wild. Cut followers down, it seemed, and more of them would spring up willy-nilly. It was a deeply self-defeating enterprise to try and stamp out the bacchic frenzy.

The enforcers were systematically cuffing and restraining maenads. Half a dozen of the others were already pinned to the ground, and now it was my turn. I couldn't believe how erotic it was. The enforcer pushed me down to the ground hard enough to leave bruises; the feeling of his fingers marking the flesh of my arms was extremely sexually arousing. Brisk humiliation compounded the effect; a second enforcer held my head down to the cold muddy ground while the first efficiently pulled my wrists together behind my back. He roughly fastened them together and pulled me upright. I was panting and felt as though my tongue must be lolling out in a sort of parody of sexual hunger; a rope of saliva fell from my mouth, and the enforcer rubbed his forearm against my chin to wipe it away, the fabric of his shirt surprisingly soft against my skin.

Our procession back to the clubhouse was quiet, ragtag. We did not want to be stopped by the police. We had to be quiet and docile as a signal to onlookers that we were going voluntarily.

Inside the clubhouse, the lighting was different than it had been before. An actual spotlight had been rigged to illuminate the central arena, giving it the feel of a boxing ring, and a circle had been marked on the floor.

All of us maenads were herded into one corner of the room. Everyone was here now. The space was warm with human heat.

Now all the lights went out at once. It was pitch black. I could feel the movement of the bodies around me, and I momentarily experienced a wave of panic. Within a minute or two, though, someone was moving among us. My wrists were lifted up and I heard the snip of shears. My hands fell free to my sides and I rubbed my left wrist with my right fingers to ease the soreness, wondering whether the plastic had actually cut into my skin or if it were just a dent pressed into the flesh. There was a sticky residue that might have been wine or blood.

Then the lights came back on. The central circle was flooded with bright white light. Around the edges the room was more dimly lit, but it was enough to see that all the imprisoned revelers had been freed. The floor around us was littered with the discarded restraints.

Ruth was seated on a raised throne at the center of the ring of light. She looked fierce, mighty, slightly mad. She had on a gilded pasteboard crown. The drummers began beating their instruments again, this time an orderly crescendo to accompany the entrance of Anna, hands still bound behind her, enforcers at her elbows.

PENTHEUS: You call yourself a god. That is ridiculous. You are no more a god than I am!

DIONYSUS: (*ignoring the guards shaking her and stabbing her sides*) It is easy for me to withstand your taunts.

ENFORCER #1: (*to* PENTHEUS) Dionysus surrendered willingly. So did the maenads, but their chains sprang off them once they were imprisoned.

**MAENADS:** (*stepping out towards the central arena and making a circle*) EVOE EVOE EVOE EVOE EVOE

**PENTHEUS:** (*to the* ENFORCER) Untie her hands.

Ruth was circling around Anna, inspecting her like a delivery of goods. The enforcer did as she had asked, and Anna stepped forward so that she and Ruth were standing face to face. Anna was in the same disheveled bacchanalian garb as all the rest of us, her wild locks tumbling over her shoulders. Ruth wore a highly tailored suit, cut for a woman but otherwise in the style of Savile Row menswear, her hair slicked back in a flat ponytail. I was struck once again by their unusual similarity as to build and coloring, and by the striking difference of the total effect produced.

**PENTHEUS:** Why are you here?

**DIONYSUS:** (*quietly, so that we had to crane to hear*) I bring the rites of Dionysus.

**PENTHEUS:** What are those rites?

**DIONYSUS:** Their secret is known only to initiates.

**PENTHEUS:** A clever answer, to make me want to know more. Do you perform these rituals in the day or by night?

**DIONYSUS:** We perform them by night —

**ALL OF US:** EVOE EVOE EVOE

**DIONYSUS:** — as darkness confers sanctity.

**PENTHEUS:** Darkness confers no sanctity, just trickery and corruption for women!

**DIONYSUS:** (*sternly*) Immoral behavior can be found in daytime also.

**PENTHEUS:** You will be punished for your vile sophistries!

**DIONYSUS:** No, *you* will be punished for your folly and impiety towards the god.

I knew more or less what was supposed to happen now, but even so, I let out a yell when a thunderclap drowned the room with noise. It was ridiculously frightening; my heart pounded in my chest, and I felt almost sick with the shock.

The drums began to pound again. It seemed like they were beating directly in my head. It was much too loud to hear anything, but I saw the enforcers throng about Anna again and take her arms and force them behind her. She looked very angry as she said something, but they just laughed at her and dragged her to Ruth's feet. Ruth bent down to speak with her, and whatever Anna said made her flinch back up and away.

Was Team Pentheus racking up more points this evening, or Team Dionysus? It was hard to say. Someone near me began to say the words Dionysus would use to indict Pentheus. *You do not know what your life is, or what you do, or who you are.* As the chant grew, Anna got to her feet and seemed to grow in stature.

*You do not know what your life is.*
**PENTHEUS:** Take her away!
*You do not know what you do.*
**PENTHEUS:** I mean it. I don't want to see her again. Or any of her followers — begone, rabble!
*You do not know who you are.*
**PENTHEUS:** Get her out of here!

And as Ruth fumed under the spotlight and Anna stared her down, we melted away in small groups. I hesitated for a moment downstairs about whether to return to the park with some of the others or perhaps stop at a bar with Claude and Jami, but in the end anything more would have seemed superfluous. I walked home quietly by myself, sore and sweaty and muddy from the night's doings. I took a quick shower and was asleep almost before I knew it. I didn't hear Ruth come in.

The next morning, I felt very strange. What were you supposed to do during the day when your nights were occupied with bacchic revelry? There was a strange disconnect between the two lives, the real life and the life of the game.

I felt weary but also strangely invigorated as I sat with a stack of student paper proposals in the café at Butler Library. In the late afternoon, I took to bed with a book. I was teaching *The Bell Jar* the coming week, but I put it down face open on the pillow next to mine and drifted off to sleep in the half-light of dusk. I woke only around eight, with a start, when Ruth knocked on the bedroom door.

**RUTH:** (*unrepentant*) Oh, were you asleep?
**ME:** (*groaning*) You are cruel.
**RUTH:** I'm not leaving for another hour or so, but I thought I'd see if you feel like walking over with me when I go. Anders already went over to fix some things about the lighting and do another liquor run.
**ME:** Sounds good to me, but I'd better have caffeine and food first.
**RUTH:** I might eat something myself.[25]
**ME:** Should we see if Anna wants to walk over with us too?

---

25. She ended up having a bowl of Kashi high-protein cereal with soy milk, the penitentially self-denying dinner she resorts to at times of especially stringent self-discipline. I couldn't find anything appetizing in the kitchen, but I ate a banana; Ruth doesn't like bananas, so it's safe for us to have them in the house.

**RUTH:** (*curtly*) I don't want to see her. No, we haven't had a fight or anything, but we're in agreement that for the duration of the game, we should have as little contact as possible while we're out of character. It diffuses the hostility, and that's the last thing we want.

**ME:** That makes sense.

*Buzzer rings.*

**ME:** Are you expecting anyone?

**RUTH:** No, definitely not. Probably it's just a food delivery guy for someone in one of the other apartments.

*Buzzer again.*

**JAMI:** (*tinnily, through the intercom*) Can I come up?

**ME:** (*to* JAMI, *once she was in the door*) What's up?

**JAMI:** (*visibly upset*) I don't know exactly. Lucy, can I talk to you?

**RUTH:** I can leave you two alone. I'm heading out shortly anyway.

**JAMI:** Actually, that didn't come out right. Ruth, I'd much prefer you to stay. It's something that concerns you also.

**RUTH:** What are you talking about?

**JAMI:** It will be easier for me to show you than tell you in words. Obviously, I don't have the password for the Pentheus threads, but I was looking on the site for something else and I bumped up against this link to a Tumblr that's pretty clearly connected with Team Pentheus. Can I show you on this computer?

**RUTH:** Be my guest.

**JAMI:** Look at this. You can see the people who post are using

Foursquare to check in at individual locations. Sometimes it's Grant's Tomb, sometimes it's the old Croton Aqueduct building on Amsterdam, sometimes it's just a street corner like 112th and Broadway. Each post on the blog just has a photograph, without any text. Look at what the pictures show.

**ME:** (*shortsightedly, without my glasses*) Is that a homeless person?

**RUTH:** (*horrified*) Yes, and his face is covered with bruises!

**JAMI:** They call each shot a "tuft." Ruth, do you know anything about this?

**RUTH:** I know nothing about it. What are you implying?

**JAMI:** We still haven't been told what Team Pentheus members are doing for points.

**RUTH:** You think — no. No way. God, no! Absolutely not.

**ME:** I still don't totally understand what you think they're doing.

**JAMI:** They're roaming the neighborhood, as I said, collecting tufts. Each tuft is a documented attack on a homeless person. Scroll down further, and you'll see that sometimes the picture shows bruising, or even the victim vomiting, probably after being punched in the stomach. In one photo you can actually see the enforcer's feet kicking the person on the ground.

**ME:** (*having retrieved my glasses and perused the pictures more closely*) This can't be real. Someone's staged it. It's an elaborate fake.

**RUTH:** (*pale*) I hope so, but I think there's a chance it's real.

**JAMI:** Of course it's real. Aren't you going to do something about it? Surely you wouldn't condone real live brutality, loyalty to Team Pentheus notwithstanding.

**RUTH:** I would never countenance violence. This has to be a rogue element. What we're doing for points — I can't disclose the details, but it has to do with scanning people's driver's licenses without them knowing. It's nothing to do with this. I'll talk to Anders and see what he knows about the tufts. If the site's genuine, I'm sure he'll know what to do.

**JAMI:** Well, you'll excuse me for being skeptical on that count, but I guess I can wait for you to talk to him before taking this any further. The police should be told, but can you imagine calling up the local precinct and trying to explain what's going on?

We felt chastened, daunted as we walked over together to the clubhouse. Ironically it was a beautiful night, not exactly warm but balmy, breezy, the scent of spring strong in the air. A few times we passed a prone figure on church steps or in an alley, and my heart beat faster, but it seemed to be the ordinary spectacle of homelessness, not a confirmation of Penthean violence.

We were pretty early, and there weren't a lot of other people there yet. Ruth immediately shut herself up in the area partitioned off at the back, saying that she needed to get into character. She asked me to tell Anders to check in with her when he returned from his errands.

By imperceptible stages, the room grew packed. Anna passed among us, stopping to share a word and a glass with each cluster of celebrants. She was still just bacchic Anna, not full-on Dionysus, though the transition had begun to be underway. It was not as dramatic as the transformation of Bruce Banner into the Hulk, there was no question of glowing eyes or green skin, but I knew that shortly I would look at her and be astonished by how little of Anna remained in the avatar before me.

The enforcers were hanging out at the other end of the space.

Anti-Dionysianism did not stop most of them from pounding liquor. I saw Anders appear at the top of the stairs and went to let him know that Ruth wanted to talk to him. He scowled, but ten minutes later he came back with a note from Ruth.

> Lucy! I think everything's OK — Anders says the pictures are fakes. We'll talk more tomorrow, but I wanted to let you know before game play begins. xR

I showed the note to Jami, and we agreed that though we couldn't take his word for it without further investigation, we would consider our concerns temporarily allayed.[26]

I'm not sure whether the timing of this was more fortunate or unfortunate, but just at that moment Anna came over to us and leaned into my shoulder, slipping me a small opaque plastic envelope and whispering into my ear that there was one hit for each of us. I unfurled the little plastic string that kept the envelope shut. Inside was a tiny sheet of perforated paper no larger than a postage stamp, printed with four little bunches of grapes. Was tripping, really and truly chemically tripping, a good idea? Especially if rogue enforcers really had started beating up the disenfranchised of Morningside Heights?

**ME:** I'm not sure we should. . . .

**JAMI:** Ten minutes ago, I'd have agreed with you, but my mind has been relieved, at least for now, and I think that's worth celebrating. I want one!

---

26. I genuinely wasn't sure at this point whether to believe Anders or not. I wanted to, but my awareness that I wanted to also made me wary. Life certainly would be *easier* if the pictures were fictional.

**CLAUDE:** Yes, so do I.

**ME:** There are four hits. Does anybody want a double?

**CLAUDE:** One full dose for each us, and a little extra.

I separated the pieces from each other, my fingers damp with oil and sweat in a way that made me imagine the drug already passing through the ridges of my prints and entering the bloodstream. We let the felt-like bits of paper dissolve under our tongues. It was of course sublimely irresponsible, but I was ready to stop worrying about tufts and relish the feeling of entering into the spirit of the game.

The music was drum and bass, the air heavy with pot smoke. I wasn't wearing a watch, so I didn't have a keen sense of the pace of time passing. Jami and Claude and everyone else around me looked very beautiful. Little bits of light caught my eye all over the room. My heart had begun to race, and I was covered with a sheen of sweat, with a strong chemical taste in my mouth that wasn't unpleasant, just noticeably metallic. The thinness of the flavor of the cheap cava I was drinking became suddenly apparent. I could see the blue veins running along the pale insides of my forearms.

It's hard to explain the state I was in. I wasn't incapable of following along rationally, but it's definitely all stranger and more confusing in my memory than any of the other nights. The lights went out suddenly and I was terrified, maybe more scared than I've ever been before in my life. The drums started, first slowly and then faster. Voices seemed to come from everywhere:

WHERE IS THE GOD?

WHERE IS DIONYSUS?

MAENADS, HEAR MY VOICE.

COME TO US NOW!

EVOE!
IT IS TIME TO SHAKE THE EARTH'S FLOOR . . .

The floor did start to shake. Earthquake? It took me a while to realize it was the maenads stamping, and then I joined my feet to theirs. The lights came partway up and we poured out of the space and down into the street as though a dike had burst. Were there fifty or eighty or a hundred of us? I couldn't say, but I felt my legs strong beneath me. I was running with Jami and Claude; we flooded down the street with the others and then into Morningside Park like a tsunami. I think we ran up the stairs to the path through the woods, but the whole park seemed infinitely bigger and stranger than I remembered, as though a world had opened up inside it. Claude reached out for my hand at one point and pulled me to a stop, clasping me to him and placing his lips gently on mine. We kissed like children, softly and with our mouths closed.

I grew up reading Mary Renault's novels about ancient Greece. I'd always wondered what it would feel like to live in that world and experience the presence of the god, as Renault's narrators do now and again. That Friday night in the park gave me a small glimpse of it. It was like being in a real-life version of *A Midsummer Night's Dream* or a grown-up version of the onward and upward sequence in the last Narnia book. It seemed impossible for limbs to tire, for thirst not to be immediately quenched with champagne and nectar.[27] Other bodies were infinitely available for entwining and entanglement.

As dawn approached, I found myself — rather more returned to

---

27. In retrospect I think the drink we called nectar was lemon-lime Gatorade. Believe it or not, I have never tasted anything so delicious in my entire life.

my senses than I would have perhaps liked — sprawled in a loose circle with Claude, Jami, and a dozen others on the cushions back at the clubhouse. I looked around and saw that every single other person was now asleep, but my own brain was still buzzing with chemical energy. All the alcohol had long since been consumed.

I disentangled myself and stood up and stretched my shoulders. I could feel the night of running and reveling in my legs, especially in the tightness of the hip flexors. I thought I might have strained some muscle or tendon running along the top of my right foot. It was time to go home.

The bars had closed at four, of course, but the night still had that Friday-into-Saturday party feel and I was pretty set on getting hold of a beer to bring me down from the last bit of the high. A supermarket or bodega would sell me beer; as you may know, the only time you can't get beer at a corner deli in New York City is between 3 a.m. and 8 a.m. on Sunday morning. It is a fairly Dionysian town.

There were as always bags of garbage here and there on the curb, empty bottles set down, and scraps of trash floating along the sidewalk, but I had the impression that even the city streets had been washed clean by the night's celebrations. Everything glistened with a beautiful clarity, the morning light so fresh and gorgeous that I — briefly, insanely — wondered why I didn't always stay up all night so as to see this hour, or else somehow reconfigure my personality so that it would be possible to get up before dawn and be outside to greet it. I thought of the Homeric phrase *rosy-fingered dawn,* and then of the impossibility of capturing any of this feeling in a good poem.[28]

---

28. Not just because of its being the modern world, but also because of my particular strengths and limitations as a poet. It is not self-criticism, only realistic self-description,

At that moment, a pitiful figure on the ground caught my eye. I was self-conscious at first about going over to look. Some poor drunk sap didn't need a do-gooder poking and prodding him to make sure he was all right. Then I visualized the pictures Jami had showed us. It will sound intolerably pretentious and self-serious, but I felt I had a responsibility to learn the truth, however troubling or inconvenient.

I stepped cautiously over the plastic trash bags of his possessions; his bags of cans and bottles had been torn open and scattered all over the sidewalk. He looked to be a black man, perhaps forty years old or perhaps sixty. I saw that he had been badly beaten. He was partly conscious; he looked up at me, his eyes confused.

**ME:** Are you all right?
**MAN ON GROUND:** (*incomprehensibly*) Mumble mumble mumble
**ME:** (*helplessly*) Who did this to you? The emergency room at St. Luke's is just down the block. Can I walk you there?

He started cursing me out, a flood of expletives and then something about men in boots that made me think of the enforcers' costumes. I didn't have any evidence that enforcers from the game had been involved in whatever happened to this man, just a strong irrational conviction. And if it were so, what about Anders? It seemed infinitely unlikely that something like this could be going on without his knowledge and assent.

I couldn't persuade the man to go to the hospital. For all I knew, he was right, and nothing I could say to them would make them treat him with respect and dignity. His injuries would heal over

---

when I say that my own gifts as a writer are narrow, lapidary, fully formed.

time, even without treatment. In the end, I gave him one of the two twenty-dollar bills I had in my pocket and walked away.

At the deli on the corner, I took the other crumpled damp twenty and bought an entire six-pack of beer, not just the single bottle I had initially envisioned. I also threw onto the counter a few other provisions to restore my balance: a liter of soda water and a peanut brittle bar whose wrapper I pulled open as the bleary-eyed clerk rang up my purchases. As I crammed pieces of it into my mouth and the sugar hit my bloodstream, I thought that it was possibly the best thing I had ever eaten.

At home, I took out a single bottle of Brooklyn Lager and placed the rest of the six-pack in the fridge. Rummaging in the cutlery drawer, though, I couldn't find a bottle opener. It was ridiculous. Usually there were at least three or four. Was I failing to see what was in front of my own eyes?

Then I remembered. We had taken a good many corkscrews and openers over to the clubhouse. How frustrating — some people can open a bottle of beer with a key or a belt buckle, or even with their teeth, but I am certainly not one of them.

The bottle in my hand was taunting me.

They would sell me an opener at the deli if I could make myself go back out, but the effort required seemed nearly insurmountable.

I set the bottle back in the fridge and looked to see if there was anything else to drink, but Ruth's bottle of freezer vodka had only a tiny dribble of thick clear fluid left in it, and there was literally nothing else, barring an ancient bottle of Baileys Irish Cream that did not meet my minimum drinkability standards.

I would have to go back out. I felt thoroughly wired, energized, despite the fatigue in my limbs, my dry eyeballs, and the escalation of my concern about the dealings of Team Pentheus. I picked up my keys and wallet, went out to the hall, and pressed the call button for the elevator.

It came almost at once, but before stepping in, I was struck by the notion that Anna and Anders might still be up. They wouldn't mind if I stopped by to borrow a bottle opener. Anders had one on his key chain, and maybe there would even be a small after party still going on in Anna's living room. I was pretty unimpressed with myself with regard to the desire for alcohol outweighing the need to hold Anders to account for the tufting business. But it wasn't the right time to ask Anders about tufts. That would have to wait until I was straight and sober.

When I knocked, there was no answer, but I could hear music playing inside. I tried the doorknob. It wasn't locked, so I let myself in and went straight to the kitchen. The counter was littered with empty bottles, but I didn't see anybody there. Nor could I find a bottle opener.

I followed the sound of the music down the hall to the living room. Through the doorway, I saw two figures on the couch. Anna and Anders. Anders on his back, Anna riding him, both naked. Anna's cry left no doubt in my mind. They were definitely having sex.

I backed slowly away from the doorway, desperately hoping they wouldn't become aware of my presence, but I must have made some sound. Anna looked up and directly at me. We held each other's gaze. Then I slipped away.

At home again, shaken, I wondered for a moment whether I'd imagined it. But it wasn't the hallucinogen. I'd come down off the drug. My senses were intact. They really had been together.

I still didn't have an opener. Beer was out, but I needed something to help me get to sleep. I rummaged through the bottles in the medicine cabinet, found an old Ambien prescription and bit off half of a ten-milligram tablet. I washed the bitter taste out of my mouth with a handful of tap water. Then I popped the other half of the pill as well. I thought I would go crazy if I couldn't get some hours of total unconsciousness.

My last waking thought was a flash of revelation that this couldn't be the first time Anna and Anders had slept with each other. Did Ruth know? No. Ruth was surely ignorant, and must remain so.

## ANNA'S APHORISMS

### The onslaught of knowledge

April 16, 2011; 7:19 a.m.

Aristotle, in the *Poetics:*

> A Discovery is, as the very word implies, a change from igno-
> rance to knowledge, and this to either love or hate, in the per-
> sonage marked for good or evil fortune.

*Posted in* Knowledge, Prohibitions

I woke up around ten. For a minute I felt happily replete, weary in my limbs but only in that satisfying way that follows a challenging workout. Then I remembered.

I had an unrealistic fantasy of not having to see Ruth at all, but when I went out into the living room after peeing and brushing my teeth, I found Ruth lying on the couch with a book open in her hand and an empty pint container of Coffee Heath Bar Crunch on the floor. She looked quite strange, but I couldn't say how much of that might be due to the aftereffect of the hallucinogen: the hollows of her eyes were dark, cavernous, and the veins ran too close to the skin, so that you could see the green and purple coursing beneath.

**ME:** Is everything all right?

**RUTH:** Not really, but there's nothing you can do about it.

**ME:** I'm still worried about tufts.

**RUTH:** So am I, a little, but I don't think we can do anything until after the game's over. I promise you I'll figure out what happened. If there's been any violence, we'll go to the police.

**ME:** Thanks.

**RUTH:** Lucy?

**ME:** What?

**RUTH:** What is it you do out there?

**ME:** In the park, you mean?

**RUTH:** Yes. What is it you do when you're in the park with the other maenads?

**ME:** You would have to be there to understand it. If I describe the things we do, it will sound wrong, lascivious. It will sound like what Pentheus thinks it is.

**RUTH:** Pentheus might be right.

**ME:** Pentheus is not right.[29]

**RUTH:** (*suspiciously*) Did Anna give you something last night?

**ME:** (*evasively*) Anna did give me something.

**RUTH:** What did she give you?

**ME:** Do you really want to know?

---

29. It is of course ridiculous to talk about literary characters as though they are real people, but I had fallen into the habit of it over the course of the game.

**RUTH:** (*seemingly oblivious to the goofy sound of our exchange*) Of course I really want to know. Why wouldn't I?

**ME:** I'm not sure you really do.

**RUTH:** Maybe you're right.

**ME:** How did Anders know the pictures on the site were fakes?

**RUTH:** Internal evidence, maybe? Actually I'm not sure. You could ask him yourself. He's just down the hall.

**ME:** (*conflict-avoidant, wretchedly*) Maybe I'll ask him tomorrow. It will be strange when the game's over, won't it? It seems as though we've been playing forever.

**RUTH:** I think we've been playing quite long enough.

**ME:** Are you scared about tonight?

**RUTH:** A little.

**ME:** What do you think will happen?

**RUTH:** I can't even guess. But I think it's important to see it through to the end. Welcome whatever the night brings.

**ME:** "What happens in Vegas stays in Vegas"?

**RUTH:** That's actually a pretty good description of the magic circle, though Anders is more interested in what happens when there's nothing that's not circle. When the circle breaks and the game bleeds out into the world.

**ME:** The broken circle — I suppose a good deal of damage can be done via spillage.

I went next door to the kitchen and ate some fruit and yogurt for breakfast. I still had little psychedelic shimmers around the edges of my field of vision, but my metabolism must have benefited from the alcohol cutoff enforced by the missing bottle opener, as I didn't feel in the least bit hungover.

What I'd seen next door was weighing on me more than tufts. I dumped my mug and bowl in the sink and retreated to the bedroom. After reading the handful of new emails in my inbox, I wrote a one-line note to Anna, the subject line just a question mark.

A response popped up immediately: "Coffee at the Hungarian, 11:30?"

I wrote back to confirm, then checked my watch. It was 10:45 already. I managed to shower and dress and get myself out the door without any more conversation.

Anna was already at the pastry shop when I got there. I ordered cherry strudel and a latte at the counter, then joined Anna at her table. She was picking at one of the luridly iced little cakes for which the shop was seminotorious. It belatedly occurred to me that in *Places of Power,* these hardy little pink and yellow decorative nubs might have been appropriately stationed all around the rim of Morningside Heights as an additional layer of occult protection.

ANNA: (*plunging straight into things*) I know you saw us together last night. You have to promise you'll keep it a secret. Anders will kill me if he finds out you know. He'll be terrified in case you say something to Ruth.

ME: What if I feel like I *should* say something to Ruth?

ANNA: (*sharply*) Do you?

ME: I don't know. I'm confused. Partly it has to do with how your brother's thinking of their relationship. If it's pretty much over, all this is really none of my business, and I'm happy to pretend I never saw a thing.

ANNA: I'm not sure even Anders himself knows whether he intends to keep going out with Ruth. I guess I'd better talk to him about it. I'm not totally unscrupulous. I have a conscience.

ME: It is a cliché, but I don't want Ruth to get hurt.

ANNA: Anyone who gets involved with my brother is likely to end up getting hurt. If there were an easy way to cut off ties with him, I'd have done it myself long ago, but he just won't leave me alone. He finds me wherever I go, however far away it is.

**ME:** Anna, do you think it's possible that some of the enforcers are committing real violence?

**ANNA:** What are you talking about?

**ME:** Do you have your phone?

**ANNA:** (*looking at the page I showed her, then putting aside the device without comment*) The game's almost over. I'll talk to Anders later this afternoon about the relationship thing. If things are over between him and Ruth, I agree, that's one thing. If he really wants a serious relationship with her, though, there are things he needs to tell her about our history.

**ME:** Things, as in sexual things?

**ANNA:** Not just sexual things. He almost killed our stepfather when he was thirteen. It was true, he'd been beating us both, but Anders has a violent streak. I can't say for sure, but the idea of tufts would fit in with that side of him. It's fine for me. I know he's not going to hurt me physically. He has a deep need for me in his life and I don't think he'll do anything to jeopardize that. But I'm worried about Ruth's vulnerability. She doesn't know him like I do.

After Anna left, I felt dirty, dirty with unwanted knowledge. On an impulse, and with full awareness of its absurdity as a response to the situation, I stopped in at the nail salon on Broadway and asked for a pedicure. It might have been fiddling while Rome burned, but it was a very pleasant sort of fiddling. The feeling of the hot water on my feet was immensely relaxing. I nearly fell asleep as I sat on the chair above the little sink and let the woman work some of the dead skin off the soles of my feet with a pumice stone. She commented on the scratches and bruises around my ankles and up my calves, and I felt as though I were holding to myself a huge armful of secrets. It was just two people having sex who shouldn't, right? There was nothing inherently shocking about that, I told myself, but it felt like the end of the world.

Ruth had already left for a photo shoot when I got home. *New York* magazine had heard about the *Bacchae* game via Twitter and wanted to include a few pictures and a short blurb in the next issue. Featured would be Ruth and Anna and Anders, all of them dressed up in clothes from the new collection of some designer whose name I can't now remember (and of course they couldn't run the pictures after what happened, so Google won't tell me either), but that had some obscure connection to Dionysus.

When she got home, Ruth was in a foul mood. The shoot had taken more time than she imagined, and left her looking not at all like herself: beautiful, but with a face covered in a near-mask of porcelain maquillage that made her resemble a shop mannequin.[30]

**RUTH:** (*miserably*) I can't go out tonight looking like this.
**ME:** Can't you just wash it off?
**RUTH:** It'll come off better if I actually shower.
**ME:** Well, there's still plenty of time, isn't there? It's only six thirty.
**RUTH:** I guess so.

---

30. I hate the smell and texture of face powder. There are few things more off-putting than the sight of powder on skin. I suppose if people would wear on the one hand delicately near-invisible makeup or on the other completely stylized and obviously artificial makeup (Daryl Hannah as Pris in *Blade Runner*!), that would be fine. But the obvious layers of foundation and powder you see on the faces of female office workers in the subway always look totally revolting to me.

I put her irritability down to nerves. Indeed, I had begun to feel almost unpleasantly keyed up myself for the final night of the game. It wasn't as acute a feeling of nervousness and adrenaline as performing in a play might have induced, but it was not wholly unrelated. As an academic type of person, I associate this sensation with taking a standardized test like the SAT, that vibe of being charged up and ready to throw yourself into what the next few hours will bring.[31]

When Ruth came out of the shower in her pristine white bathrobe, she had a towel wrapped around her hair. I was surprised she hadn't cared to hold on to the stylist's beautifully sleek blown-out look.

**RUTH:** I couldn't get all the makeup off my face without washing my hair as well. I'm going to slick it back again in any case. You won't believe what they did to Anna. They blew her hair completely straight. It looked amazing, but not at all like her. You know how those snaky curls of hers are almost the only thing you notice about her sometimes?

**ME:** Anna with straight hair! Will she leave it like that for tonight?

**RUTH:** She really needs those snake locks writhing around her head to play Dionysus properly, but it looked pretty awesome. If I were her, I'd definitely keep the look.

In the bathroom, I changed into maenad garb. My own face in the mirror looked depressingly ordinary. I put on some dark eyeliner, more eye shadow than I usually wear and a sharp line of

---

31. It is mortifying to admit that taking the SAT is the most Dionysian experience I can remember.

bright red lipstick, a Chanel one I'd bought in the duty-free store coming back from a writers' conference in Belize. There was nothing much to be done about my hair, which is black, chin length and thick to the point of bushiness. There was no chance of my being able to tether any greenery into it or arrange it in the kind of dramatic spilling-out upsweep some of the other girls wore.

My computer pinged.

| jami | can u come early to help fix leaves on wands |
| lucy | sure |
| lucy | but not very handy |
| jami | no worries |
| jami | have tools |
| jami | picked up leaves and branches at wholesale florist earlier |
| jami | havent slept since last night |
| jami | thought wands were looking a little pitiful |
| jami | figured they could use sprucing up |
| lucy | be there in 15 min |

Before leaving, I checked as always for keys and emergency money. There would almost certainly be plenty to drink, but it was worth having an extra twenty in case I needed to buy a bottle of wine or a couple of drinks at a bar. I called out to Ruth that I'd see her over there; she shouted back something incomprehensible from the bathroom as I walked out the door.

The feeling of it being Saturday night was strong in the air as I walked across to Morningside Drive, down the steps into the park and over to Manhattan Avenue. Everyone I saw seemed to have a bottle hidden in a brown paper bag. The secret brotherhood of

Bacchus is alive and well in 2011 in New York City. Even Mayor Giuliani, with all his cracking down on street offenses, hadn't been able to change human nature, and Bloomberg had no hope: the urge to guarantee a safe, personal liquor supply is one of those traits even a Robespierre or a Stalin can't expect to extinguish.

At the clubhouse, a section of the floor was covered with the fronds Jami and a few others were weaving onto the short poles we used as wands. I went to help them, and with lots of pairs of hands we finished fairly quickly, freeing us up to lounge on cushions and get started on the evening's alcohol consumption. A few glasses of wine made me feel light and free and ready to absorb whatever the last night of the game would bring.

By nine, the room was mostly full. There were more people than ever before. I saw a pack of enforcers I was sure I'd never laid eyes on in my life. Team Dionysus continued to dominate by dint of sheer numbers. The lights were low, the music loud, and the drinking had by now been long enough underway that the buzz of conversation had become a cacophony.

We had a chant, its cadence vaguely reminiscent of Queen's "We Will Rock You":

THERE IS NO GOD GREATER THAN DIONYSUS
HONOR US WITH YOUR PRESENCE
THERE IS NO GOD GREATER THAN DIONYSUS
THERE IS NO GOD GREATER THAN DIONYSUS

We had probably repeated it several dozen times, maybe even more like a hundred, when the figure of Dionysus appeared at the back of the room. It was Anna, of course, but Anna unrecognizable. She wore a sort of headdress, an armature of branches and greenery that gave her the look of an Egyptian pharaoh, her bronze oiled skin gleaming under the lights. When she raised her hands, the whole room roared in appreciation.

THERE IS NO GOD GREATER THAN DIONYSUS

Dionysus took up her place at the edge of the circle. Though the drumming continued, our voices seemed to die down as Pentheus made her entrance. Her limbs were pale, moon-like in contrast to Dionysus' glow. She wore a tunic, plain light gray and loosely cut, her knees bare beneath it, her feet in gladiator-style sandals whose straps went halfway up her calves. Her dark hair was pomaded back and tied in a ponytail at the nape of the neck.

She walked straight up to Dionysus and stopped directly across from her.

NO GOD IS GREATER THAN DIONYSUS

said someone in a quiet voice from the other side of the room.

The rest of us took up the chant, and the noise grew:

THERE IS NO GOD GREATER THAN DIONYSUS
THERE IS NO GOD GREATER THAN DIONYSUS
**THERE IS NO GOD GREATER THAN DIONYSUS**

Dionysus struck the floor with her staff and called for silence. Enforcers were glowering at revelers, but had done nothing thus far to censor the celebrations. They simply stood and watched in small groups, menacing in their dark uniforms and heavy boots.

**DIONYSUS:** You will not be permitted to march against the maenads.
**PENTHEUS:** Spare me the lectures!
**DIONYSUS:** You and your enforcers will be put to flight, your shields turned aside by the maenads' wands.

**PENTHEUS:** (*to the crowd*) I am locked in combat with this stranger. She will not keep silent!

**DIONYSUS:** We can settle this matter sensibly between us. If Team Pentheus can do something that will make all sexual contact cease — if you can produce a sex-free zone in Morningside Park tonight — if you can stop *anybody* and *everybody* from having sex during a timed and agreed-upon one-hour interval, Team Pentheus will count tonight a great victory. There must be no kissing, no penetration, no contact between mouth and skin, and you must use persuasion rather than violence. Any form of verbal abuse or berating is permissible. You can say unforgivable things, anything that you think will separate one partner from another. But you're not allowed to touch members of the opposing team with your hands.

**PENTHEUS:** Not with our hands, but with our words we will touch them.

**DIONYSUS:** The interval starts at midnight precisely. What your followers do before then is their own business; the only time period that will be counted is the stretch from midnight to one a.m. But first, a boon. You want to see the maenads out in the woods, don't you?

**PENTHEUS:** I suppose I would like to see them.

**DIONYSUS:** You didn't want to see them before.

**PENTHEUS:** (*self-righteously*) Of course I didn't want to see them drunk.

**DIONYSUS:** You don't want to see them drinking and fucking?

**PENTHEUS:** Well, I wouldn't mind seeing them, so long as they couldn't see that I was watching.

**DIONYSUS:** You shall go openly, and I will be your guide. But first you must do something for me.

**PENTHEUS:** I will do what you request.

**DIONYSUS**: You must dress like one of my worshipers, so that they cannot say you do not belong.

And a couple of maenads stepped up and pulled the tunic off Pentheus. She had on very little underneath, just a flesh-colored sports bra and a pair of nude underpants that matched her skin closely enough that you almost would have sworn she wasn't wearing anything at all. Two other girls ran forward carrying fawnskin, wand, and headband with greenery. They draped it all as carefully over Pentheus as if they were crafting a museum exhibit, pressing the thyrsus into her hand as the final touch.

Dionysus stepped forward to make a minute adjustment to the fawnskin. The two figures looked almost identical now, headgear and clothing masking their minute differences. I saw Dionysus — Anna — lean over and say something into the ear of Pentheus. It was impossible to guess what the words were, but Ruth nodded.

I was in full possession of my faculties at this point, or at least as fully in possession of them as was compatible with having already had three or four drinks and intending to consume at least as many more before the night was over.

Dionysus led us along the avenue to the park entrance, disappearing from view ahead of me (I was running near the back of the pack). All we had to do between now and midnight was tread the ground in ecstasy, watch whatever spectacle was on offer and have as much sex as we could.

The first thing I did was run up the hill to the left and into the woods, Jami and Claude and two or three others behind me. One man had concealed a bottle of wine beneath his clothing, and we shared it between us, drinking from the mouth of the bottle and cackling as it spilled over our faces and necks. Everywhere you looked there were tangled limbs, strange configurations of bodies pressed up against rocks and trees.

Something was happening. People were gathering not far from us in a wide flat area that gave a good line of sight on the little crenellated viewing platform up high above on Morningside Drive at the rim of the park. It must have been hundreds of feet higher than us, because of that marked rise in elevation that characterizes the topography of the whole area. They had lights — were they running off a car battery? — and Dionysus and Pentheus appeared in a bright tableau.

We had migrated down to join the others. All around us the drumming grew louder and faster, with bits of chanting and yelling. I saw one man going down on another, and not ten yards away from me another couple were actually having all-out sex. The enforcers mostly stood around the edge of the group, muttering to each other and glaring with theatrical disapproval upon all the sexual activity as it caught their attention.

The lit platform above us was so far away, like a miniature peepshow. A third figure appeared, a man in black. Was it Anders? The two women in their fawnskins were miked. Anders wasn't. He said something to one of the women, and it speaks to their physical similarity that I couldn't at first tell which one it was. But it must have been Anna, and when she stepped towards him and spoke, it wasn't in her Dionysus voice.

**ANNA:** I've made my decision. I'm going to tell Ruth everything.
**ANDERS:** (*gripping her arm and twisting it behind her back*) If you do —
**RUTH:** (*to Anders*) Stop that! What are you doing?
**ANDERS:** Shut up!

We had all gone still, hushed. Even now that we were near silent, it was difficult to catch the unamplified words, and we strained to hear them. The pretense of the Greek fiction — of the game itself — had fallen suddenly and entirely away. It was just two identical female figures in fawnskins, Anders between them.

The voice that came forth from Anna's throat next was somehow once again the voice of Dionysus. It had an absolute authority.

ANNA: (*speaking to Anders, but taking Ruth's hand*) Get away from me. I never want to see you again.

ANDERS: (*forcing his way back in between the two women*) You're not going to get away with this!

RUTH: (*trying to separate them*) No! This is all wrong. Stop it, Anders! If you're not careful, she'll —

ANDERS: (*turning and pushing Ruth instead*) Think about what you're doing —

SPECTATOR #1: Not so close to the edge!

SPECTATOR #2: Be careful, man! Do you know —

SPECTATOR #3: Isn't anyone else up there? Get them the hell down from that wall!

It was not so much a human figure as a fawn-colored splodge that I saw descend through the air. Out of the tangle of three bodies pressed right up to the hip-height wall, one light-colored projectile flew over the edge with enough force to fall well clear of wall and cliff on the hard ground far below.

I was the first person to break our paralysis and start running to the spot where she had fallen. I couldn't stop yelling her name.

RUTH RUTH RUTH

Nobody could have survived that fall without massive injury. Bodies are so easily broken. I was pierced suddenly with the thought of my mother's limp shell in the hospital bed.

I fought through the undergrowth and fell to the ground beside the body. It lay prone on top of the dirt, cloth torn away from the shoulders to reveal flesh-toned underwear. The dark, straight locks of her hair poured over her shoulders, and her arms were extended in front of her as though she were trying to crawl away from the stone walk where she had landed.

It wasn't Ruth. It was Anna, Anna with her hair straightened, Anna whose brother hadn't wanted her to tell.

I was afraid to touch her.

**ME:** Anna? Anna, are you all right?

The broken person on the ground made no response. I took her wrist very gently and felt for a pulse. Her arm was completely limp. There was no pulse. I leaned over and put my head to Anna's chest to try and tell if she was still breathing. There was no breath. The spirit had left the body.

The game was over, I thought.

I was wrong. There was one more move to come.

**Morningside Metro (morningsidemetro.com)**

**Sunday, April 17, 2011**
**MTA Reporting Delays on A/C Train Due To Police Activity At Cathedral Parkway**

According to the Morningside Metro advisory at 1:51 a.m.:

We have been advised by the MTA that due to police activity at the Cathedral Parkway Station, A/C Train service on the downtown line is suspended until further notice.

An update from the MTA at 6:50 a.m. reports that regular A/C subway service has been restored.

**UPDATE** 9:50 a.m. —

An unidentified man was fatally struck by a southbound A train as it entered the Cathedral Parkway station at approximately 11:50 p.m. last night. The victim was pronounced dead at the scene.

**BREAKING NEWS** 11:10 a.m. —

The victim has been identified as Anders Stavros Ekman, 35, wanted for questioning in the suspicious death of Anna Ekman, 34. The incident occurred shortly before midnight in Morningside Park, in what police are calling a live-action role-playing game that ended in tragedy.

COMMENTS (4)

**Citycommenter**       4/17/2011 9:55 AM

Assholes like this shouldn't mess up other people's travel plans. This guy shoulda gone and offed himself somewhere else.

**RaLaCuBa13**  4/17/2011 9:58 AM

You are considerate!

**BikeGuy1966**  4/17/2011 10:03 AM

I was there on the platform. Not a suicide IMO. I talked to the guy just minutes before he went over the edge. He asked if the A would take him to JFK. I said yes, if he didn't mind it taking a hell of a long time. He laughed (he was pretty wound up) and said he wasn't in a hurry. He spoke good English, but definitely not from the United States. Northern European, maybe? Then two police detectives came through the turnstiles and started to approach him. He backed away from them. They didn't caution him or anything, just rushed him and grabbed his arms. Guy pulled away and fell back onto the tracks. Train was already approaching. Nothing any of us could do.

**Mikeymike11**  4/17/2011 11:15 AM
I was there too. Total horror show. One guy, multiple body bags. I saw one EMT throw up on the tracks. Other EMT said head completely severed from the body.

# CODA: JULY 2012

| jami | hey |
| lucy | havent seen u online for a while |
| jami | wanna go to yoga tomorrow am? |
| lucy | im in brooklyn now |
| jami | whoa |
| jami | you had such a sweet deal uptown |
| lucy | ruth gave up the lease |
| lucy | i had to move out |
| jami | hows ruth? |
| lucy | havent talked to her recently |
| jami | ? |
| lucy | she went to san francisco |
| lucy | gave up her postdoc and left academia |
| lucy | working at a nonprofit |
| jami | well if you talk to her tell her i say hey |
| lucy | ok |
| lucy | do you think about the game? |
| jami | yeah wish it ended differently |

| | |
|---|---|
| lucy | any other ending would have been better |
| lucy | well maybe not any other |
| lucy | but you know what i mean |
| jami | i still dont really understand what happened |
| lucy | me neither |
| jami | where was anders going? |
| lucy | airport id guess |
| jami | wouldnt have thought hed kill himself |
| jami | even with cops on his tail |
| jami | i guess even though he was the one that pushed her he couldnt live w/o her |
| lucy | something like that |
| jami | ruth isnt still facing legal charges is she? |
| lucy | no |
| lucy | family lawyer made problems go away |
| lucy | and really it would have been stupid to charge her |
| lucy | everybodys fault and nobodys |
| jami | i keep thinking about his head |
| lucy | ugh i know |
| lucy | so gross |
| lucy | some kind of poetic justice |
| jami | like he got what he deserved? |
| lucy | too harsh maybe |
| lucy | i always thought at the end of the bacchae that pentheus secretly wanted to lose his head |
| lucy | its his mother who gets a rough deal |
| lucy | she has to live with what she did |
| lucy | even if she wasnt in her right mind when she did it |

| | |
|---|---|
| jami | but ruth was trying to stop anders pushing her over |
| jami | youre not saying she blames herself |
| lucy | i dont know what she does or doesnt do |
| lucy | she prob doesnt know herself |
| lucy | line in lear i always loved |
| lucy | he hath ever slenderly but known himself |
| lucy | ruth has ever slenderly but known herself |
| lucy | recipe for a tragedy |
| jami | deep! |
| jami | so, yoga? |
| lucy | no thanks |
| lucy | too lazy |
| lucy | only thing i can do is lie in bed and read a book |
| lucy | cant write my thesis |
| lucy | cant stop thinking about what happened |
| lucy | cant see how to get past it |
| lucy | the moment of the fall |
| lucy | the plummet |
| lucy | the broken body |
| lucy | the end |

# NOTE ON SOURCES

Passages from Euripides' *The Bacchae* are quoted (and in some cases freely adapted) from John Davie's translation, in *The Bacchae and Other Plays,* intro. Richard Rutherford (London: Penguin, 2005).

I consulted too many books about games to cite them all here, but I am particularly indebted to Markus Montola, Jaakko Stenros, and Annika Waern's indispensable volume *Pervasive Games: Theory and Design* (Burlington, MA: Elsevier/Morgan Kaufmann, 2009) and to Johanna Koljonen's essay "'I Could a Tale Unfold Whose Lightest Word Would Harrow up Thy Soul': Lessons from *Hamlet,*" available online at http://www.ropecon.fi/brap/ch18 .pdf.

Andrew Dolkart's *Morningside Heights: A History of Its Architecture and Development* (New York: Columbia University Press, 1998) was an inspiration on many points, and so was Julius Chambers' 1876 book-length exposé of abuses at the Bloomingdale Asylum, *A Mad World and Its People.*

# ACKNOWLEDGMENTS

Several things prompted me to write this book: teaching *The Bacchae* more than ten years ago in the Literature Humanities sequence at Columbia was one; another was participating as an interpreter in two pieces of Tino Sehgal's, "This Situation" at the Marian Goodman Gallery and "This Progress" at the Guggenheim. Thanks are due not just to Tino but to Louise Höjer, Asad Raza and all of my fellow players. I am as always grateful to my Columbia students and colleagues for providing a stimulating and conversable atmosphere for life and work in Morningside Heights.

A few years ago, I wanted to write a book about forms of culture that can only be transmitted directly from one person to another by gesture rather than through language. I no longer believe I will write such a book, but some of that thinking colored my writing here, and I'd like to thank the swimming and yoga teachers whose knowledge and instruction fed into that preoccupation.

My editor, Ed Park, was so imaginative and patient in his suggestions that in a just world, he'd have a co-author credit on this book. As it is, I can only give him my most heartfelt and extravagant thanks. I am also grateful to the entire team at Amazon's literary fiction imprint and to Kathleen Anderson for finding my book such a good home.

Thanks are undoubtedly due to many others I don't have the wherewithal to name here, but particularly to family and friends who tolerated the antisocial behavior that seems to accompany novel writing. I got various good suggestions from members of the semi-secret Internet cabal, and am especially grateful to Sherri Wasserman; Lauren Klein read an early draft and educated me on matters concerning Apple and climbing in particular, saving me from a few potentially mortifying missteps. Remaining mistakes and misapprehensions are all my own.

The person to whom I owe deepest thanks is Brent Buckner, who educated me about games and gaming with persistence and good humor. He introduced me to *Firefly* and *Serenity,* showed me the classic D&D scene at the end of *Freaks and Geeks* and the documentaries *Darkon* and *The King of Kong,* and made sure I watched *Ghostbusters* from start to finish, politely concealing his horror and amazement that I'd never seen it before.